PROTECTION DETAIL

SHIRLEE McCoy

D0311638

HARLEQUIN® LOVE INSPIRED® SUSPENSE

Special thanks and acknowledgment are given to
Shirlee McCoy for her contribution to the Capitol K-9 Unit miniseries

Recycling programs
for this product may
not exist in your area.

 LOVE INSPIRED BOOKS

ISBN-13: 978-0-373-44654-4

Protection Detail

www.Harlequin.com

Printed in U.S.A.

"Call off your dog!" the perp shouted. "You don't, and the woman gets it first, then the mutt."

"Cease!" Gavin commanded Glory, not because he was afraid of the threat. Glory could take the guy down in seconds. He was afraid of how much damage could be done to Cassie in those heartbeats of time it took his partner to lunge.

Glory settled onto her haunches, her dark gaze glued to the perp. She was ready. Gavin was ready.

Was Cassie?

He met her eyes. Not even a hint of terror in her dark green gaze.

The perp shifted, the gun pressed deeply into Cassie's flesh. "Open the door!" he commanded.

Cassie reached for the knob and eased the door open. But something in her face, something in the complete and utter stillness of her expression, warned Gavin that she had no intention of walking outside.

* * *

CAPITOL K-9 UNIT:
These lawmen solve the toughest cases
with the help of their brave canine partners

Aside from her faith and her family, there's not much **Shirlee McCoy** enjoys more than a good book! When she's not teaching or chauffeuring her five kids, she can usually be found plotting her next Love Inspired Suspense story or wandering around the beautiful Inland Northwest in search of inspiration. Shirlee loves to hear from readers. If you have time, drop her a line at shirlee@shirleemccoy.com.

Visit the Author Profile page at Harlequin.com for more titles

Remind me each morning of Your constant love, for I put my trust in You. My prayers go up to You; show me the way I should go. I go to You for protection, Lord; rescue me from my enemies. You are my God; teach me to do Your will. Be good to me and guide me on a safe path.
—*Psalms* 143:8-10

To the 2015 LIS continuity team—you ladies are the best!

ONE

Something pulled Cassie Danvers from the half sleep she'd fallen into and yanked her back into the world of foster children and fevers, of long nights with sick kids. She eased away from little David's bed, standing on legs that ached from too many hours sitting in one position. Five days and six nights of dealing with the eight-year-old's illness had taken its toll. She was exhausted.

A soft thump sounded from somewhere below, and she cocked her head to the side, listening for whatever would come next. Something would. She was sure of that. She'd been house mom at All Our Kids foster home for enough years to know that kids didn't always stay in bed. When it came to the kind of kids she dealt with, they often didn't.

Someone was up. Probably Destiny. The thirteen year-old had been neglected for ten years before she'd arrived at the home. As a result, she had food issues. As in, she liked to take food, hide it, hoard it. If she was up raiding the kitchen, she'd have to be dealt with. Too bad, because Cassie was just tired enough to want to ignore the issue.

She touched David's forehead. Cool as a cucumber. Finally.

That was good news and might mean they both got a good night's sleep. After Cassie got Destiny back into bed.

She hurried into the hall, tiptoeing past the boys' room. The stairs creaked as she crept to the lower level of the house. A large foyer opened out into a living room area on one side and a formal dining room on the other. Unless they had special guests, the eat-in kitchen was always a better choice for meals. More relaxed and comfortable, it offered Cassie's charges a chance to sit down and get a feel for what it meant to be part of a family. Or, in some cases, to remember what it felt like.

A wide hall stretched from the foyer to the back of the house. The family room and kitchen were there. The two most tempting areas for Cassie's foster kids. TV and video games in the family room. Food in the kitchen. Not to mention the back door. That had tempted a few too many kids to wander outside unattended. She'd put a bolt at the top, but that couldn't keep the more clever and persistent kids from escaping.

Fortunately, Destiny wasn't one to wander. She'd been through way too much in her thirteen years, and she preferred to stay as close to All Our Kids as possible. Food, though, that was her weakness.

Cassie made her way down the hall, passing photos of dozens of children who'd spent time in the home. Some were kids who'd come and gone before she'd become housemother. Most were her kids. Hers for a while, anyway. She tried not to get melancholy about loving and saying goodbye to so many. Sometimes, though, she wanted to be more than someone's foster mom. Sometimes, she wanted to be Mommy, Mom, Mother.

The hallway emptied out into the family room and

kitchen area. The rooms were dark, and she didn't turn on the light. If Destiny was hanging around somewhere, it was best to catch her in the act. Otherwise, Cassie would have to spend the rest of the night trying to get the kid to own up to her mistakes.

She glanced around the kitchen. No sign of Destiny. No telltale candy wrappers on the counter. She looked in the trash can. No chip bags. That didn't mean much. Destiny had been known to take her contraband food out onto the back porch, sit in the hanging swing and munch to her heart's content. Cassie might have been tempted to allow her to do it, but Destiny was a kid who needed clear rules and firm boundaries. Snacks were fine if the kids were hungry. They weren't fine in the middle of the night and in massive quantities.

Cassie crept to the door. The bolt wasn't locked, and she really hoped Destiny had been the one to slide it open. Some of the other kids weren't as likely to stay close to the house. She grabbed the doorknob, careful to make as little noise as possible. She'd learned the hard way that Destiny was great at hiding evidence, making up stories and pretending that she was as innocent as a newborn baby. Right at that moment, Cassie wasn't in the mood for it.

The doorknob barely turned. Locked. Had Destiny locked herself outside?

Cassie turned the lock and swung the door open, expecting to see Destiny sitting on the swing, a bag of chips in her hands and a guilty look on her face. Instead, she looked into a stranger's cold blue eyes, his hard face.

She screamed, the sound bursting out of her as she jumped backward and tried to slam the door shut. He grabbed it, grabbed *her*, yanking her out onto the porch.

She pulled against his hold, and screamed again, the acrid scent of gasoline filling her nose.

She fought, because it was what she'd grown up doing, scraping an existence in the meanest neighborhood DC had to offer. She punched the stranger in the stomach, swung again. He backhanded her so hard she fell onto the swing, that horrible gasoline scent making her dizzy.

"Cool it!" the guy growled as he hefted an oversize duffle with one hand and reached under his jacket with the other.

She didn't know what he was reaching for, didn't care.

All she cared about was warning the kids, warning her assistant, Virginia Johnson. She screamed again, loudly enough to wake the dead.

The guy yanked a knife out from under his jacket, the long blade making Cassie's blood run cold.

"Scream again," he said emotionlessly, his eyes cold. "I dare you."

She didn't, because she knew the look in his eyes. She'd seen it in the eyes of more people than she'd wanted to admit. It was the look of apathy, the gaze of someone who didn't care. Dead. That's how she'd describe it, and that scared her more than the knife.

A light went on inside the house, capturing the guy's attention for the split second Cassie had been waiting for. She scrambled off the swing, sprinting off the porch, nothing else in her mind except leading the guy away from the house and the kids.

Michael Jeffries was dead, and there wasn't one thing Capitol K-9 Unit Captain Gavin McCord could do about it. It seemed inconceivable, impossible, but it was true. Michael had been a good guy, a great attorney. Fair-

minded, reasonable and determined to always see justice done. Now he was gone, shot down in the prime of his life.

That hurt. A lot.

Gavin snapped a picture of the bloodstain on the pavement at the rear of Congressman Harland Jeffries's mansion. He'd already had the evidence team collect samples for DNA. He knew they'd find DNA matching Michael Jeffries and his father. Like Michael, Harland had been shot by a small caliber handgun.

Unlike his father, the young lawyer hadn't survived.

Sad. All the way around.

Gavin knew and liked both of the men, but he couldn't let his emotions get in the way of the investigation. He snapped another picture, glanced around the scene. The DC police had been the first responders, and several officers were huddled together discussing the case. He knew most of them. He'd worked as a DC police officer for ten years before taking the job Margaret Meyer had offered him. It had been an opportunity he couldn't pass up, one that he hadn't *wanted* to pass up. He'd been working as part of the Capitol K-9 Team ever since.

Glory shifted beside him. The three-year-old shepherd was too well trained to stand before she was told to, but it was obvious that the excitement of the crime scene was making her antsy.

"Be patient," he said, touching her head as he took another photo.

Harland had been conscious when the ambulance arrived, and had given some limited information to the responding officers. Gavin would go to the hospital and interview him later. For now, he needed to concentrate on making sure that evidence was collected, the scene

processed. The more thorough they were at this stage of the game, the more likely a conviction would be later on down the road.

"McCord!" One of the DC officers stepped from the group and waved him over. Tall with dark eyes and short-cropped hair, Dane Winthrop had been a veteran officer the year Gavin left the DC police. They'd run into each other quite a few times in the years since then.

"What's up?" he asked, approaching Dane, his gaze jumping to the bloodstained concrete where Harland had been lying. Michael's body had been found a few feet away. Both areas were cordoned off, yellow crime-scene tape strung around trees and porch railings.

"One of my men found something near the tree line. I thought you might want to see it." Dane held up an evidence bag with a bright blue mitten in it. "Thing was clean as a whistle. Not a leaf on it. Not a stick. Not a speck of grass covering it."

"It looks like a kid's mitten," he said, taking the bag and turning it over.

"A small kid's," Dane agreed. "There was no tag on it. Looks like something someone's grandmother might have made."

It did. "Where was it found?"

"A few feet from the path that leads to that foster home next door. All Our Kids?"

Gavin knew it better than most. He'd lived in the home during his last two years of high school.

"Want to show me?" he asked, and Dane led the way to the woods that edged Harland's property. Wide and well used, the path was easy to find. A man and woman searched the area nearby, their K-9 partners sniffing the

ground. Glory wanted in on the action, her lean body tense with anticipation. She'd get her chance soon.

"Here's where it was." Dane pointed to a couple of bushes that sat near the tree line. A small evidence flag poked out from the ground. Gavin stood close to it and glanced toward Harland's house. A clear view of the back patio and the area where the congressman had been found.

He crouched so that he was closer to child-size. Still a clear view. The outside lights had been on. If a child had been standing where the mitten was when the shooting occurred, he or she would have seen everything.

"What do you think?" Dane asked, his hands shoved deep in his jacket pockets, his gaze on the house. He was asking, but he knew. They had a potential witness, and the thought of that sent a wave of adrenaline coursing through Gavin.

"Did you send someone over to All Our Kids?"

"Not yet. It's your case, your call. You want to go over or do you want me to?"

"I'll go." His boss, Margaret Meyer, had assigned him the case. As head of the president's special in-house security team, she'd put Capitol K-9 together and was the hub of the organization. The fact that a congressman had been shot and his son killed had been enough for her to want Capitol K-9 involved. Gavin had asked to lead the case. He'd known the Jeffries for years, owed Harland a lot, was determined to make sure Michael's killer was brought to justice. He walked to the path, eyeing the dark edges of the woods. If he were a young kid running from a killer, would he go home or hide?

Probably home, but Gavin didn't want to take any chances. Glory was trained in apprehension. Part of that

training was scent tracking. He opened the evidence bag, bent so that Glory could get a whiff of the mitten. Her ears perked, her eyes sharpened with interest.

"Find!" he commanded, and she lunged toward the trees, loped onto the path. He ran behind her, the lead loose in his hand.

Moonlight filtered through the thick tree canopy, casting golden-yellow light across dead leaves and winter-dry undergrowth. Spring hadn't quite made its appearance, the early March air frigid with winter's last sting. If a child was out in this, he'd be cold, tired, scared.

Glory veered off the path, plunging through undergrowth and between trees. She didn't hesitate. She had the scent, and she'd follow it to her mark.

She stopped a dozen feet off the path, nose to the ground, snuffling a pile of leaves. She circled a large oak, found her way onto the path again. Gavin had walked this way so many times when he was a teen that he could have done it blindfolded.

Glory paused again, cocked her head to the side and growled low in her throat.

Bushes rustled, twigs snapped.

Gavin grabbed his light and flashed it into the trees.

Nothing. Not even a hint of movement, but Glory growled again, her entire body tense, her muscles taut.

Criminal or kid. That was Gavin's guess.

"Police!" he called. "Come on out!"

Nothing.

"You come out or I'll send my dog in," he warned.

Nothing.

Okay. Fine. They'd do it the hard way.

"Track!" he issued the command, and Glory lunged

off the path, shoving through thick foliage, her wild bark ringing through the cold March air. He called in his location as he followed.

Up ahead, feet pounded on dead leaves. Whoever it was was heading toward the road. He wouldn't make it. Not before Glory caught up.

"Track!" he urged again, and Glory howled her response. She loved the chase almost as much as she loved the find.

Somewhere nearby, sirens screamed.

Another emergency?

Not uncommon in DC's rougher areas, but in the Jeffrieses' posh neighborhood, crime was nearly nonexistent.

Glory stopped short, her ears perked, her scruff standing on end. She swiveled, turning in the direction they'd come. Gavin could still hear branches breaking in front of them, but Glory was trained in protection. She wouldn't move toward a fleeing threat if there was another threat coming up from behind.

She growled, her dark eyes focused on the trees behind them. Gavin aimed his light in that direction, saw a shadow darting through the trees.

"Stop!" he shouted. "Police!"

The shadow kept going.

"I'm releasing my dog!" he yelled.

He unclipped Glory's lead, gave her the command.

She lunged into the trees, muscle and fur and enough power to take down a grown man. She wouldn't. Not until she was given the command, but she'd be able to corner whoever it was, keep him or her from escaping.

He ran after her, sprinting into the dense foliage, heading back the way they'd come. He hit the path at a

dead-out run, his light bouncing across dirt and leaves, splashing over Glory and her mark. Small. Wearing jeans and T-shirt. A woman or a kid. Long hair, so he'd say female.

The rest of the details were lost as she veered off the path, ran into the trees. She must have thought she could lose Glory that way.

Wasn't going to happen.

The woman screamed, the sound cut off by leaves rustling and Glory's wild bark.

Gavin sprinted forward, his light bouncing off Glory's brown-black coat.

"Release!" he commanded, and she moved to his side. She'd stay there until he told her differently.

"You may as well come down," he said, moving the beam of his light into the tree. It flitted over bare feet, jean-clad legs, a soft pink sweater. A face he knew well. Cassie Danvers—housemother at All Our Kids for the past couple of years. He'd done his share of volunteer work at All Our Kids. He'd owed the congressman and the home that. Last year, he'd put new tile flooring in the kitchen, painted the trim of a dozen windows, helped run a field day for foster kids and their families. He'd seen Cassie there more times than he could count.

He scowled. "What are you doing up there, Cassie?"

"Climbing for my life," she responded, her dark green gaze fixed on Glory.

Glory barked, and Cassie scrambled higher into the tree.

"Glory isn't going to hurt you."

"You might want to tell her that," she said. She had a bruise on her cheek, blood on her feet. Something had happened to send her out into the woods at this time of

the night. Had she heard the sirens? Come to see what was going on? Run into whoever it was Glory had been chasing through the woods?

He needed to get her out of the tree, get her back to All Our Kids, find out exactly what was going on.

"I already did. That's why she backed off," he responded, clipping on Glory's lead. "She won't move again unless I tell her to."

"I'm not sure I can move, either," she muttered.

"You're stuck?"

"Maybe." She peered down at him, her red hair falling across her cheeks, her eyes wide with fear. She'd managed to climb up ten feet, and he thought she might be wondering how she was going to get down.

"Want me to climb up?" he asked.

"I can figure it out. Thanks." She eased down through the tree, her hand grasping branches and pine needles.

It seemed to take forever, every painstaking inch of progress making Gavin want to climb up and give her the help she said she didn't need.

Instead, he waited.

He'd known Cassie for a couple of years. Not well, but enough to understand a few things about her. She wasn't the kind of person who liked needing help, wasn't the kind who'd trust quickly or easily. She was great with the kids, seemed to have a good relationship with Harland and Michael. She attended fund-raisers and hobnobbed with ease, but she didn't ask for anything from anyone. If one of her kids had a need, she found a way to provide for it.

That was probably one of the reasons Harland had hired her at such a young age. The go-getter attitude

combined with compassion. Those things were necessary for the job she did.

What was necessary for *his* job was information, and he needed it sooner rather than later. Because, someone else had been out in the woods with them. Someone Glory had been tracking. Someone who'd been beelining it toward the road.

Michael's killer?

Maybe.

And, maybe Cassie had seen him, could offer a description that would help bring him to justice.

Gavin needed whatever information she had.

First, though, he needed her out of the tree.

TWO

Cassie hadn't climbed a tree in years. That hadn't seemed to be a problem when she'd seen Gavin's dog coming after her. She'd scrambled up the tree so quickly, she might have broken the sound-speed barrier.

The problem was, she'd never *ever* climbed *down* a tree.

The last time she'd tried, she'd been twelve. The effort had resulted in a broken arm and a trip to the ER.

She didn't plan to repeat the mistake.

On the other hand, her progress was so slow, the sun might come up before she actually made it to the ground.

"Cassie?" Gavin called, a hint of impatience in his voice. She didn't know what he'd been doing out in the woods, but she was glad he had been. She wasn't sure how much longer she could have eluded the guy who'd been chasing her. She'd been fast, but he'd been savvy, slipping through the trees after her. Stealthy. Practiced. As if he'd hunted prey hundreds of times before.

She shuddered, her feet slipping off the bough she'd clambered onto.

"Careful," Gavin called as if she needed to be reminded that she was up in a tree, the ground a good seven feet below her.

"I'm trying," she muttered, inching down a little farther. Sirens were blaring, the sound coming from the direction of the house.

Virginia must have heard her scream and called the police.

Good. The kids would be protected.

That was all she cared about.

That and making sure the guy she'd seen on the back porch didn't return.

She stepped onto another bough, pine needles digging into her raw feet. Her cheek throbbed, her jaw ached, but she was alive, help was at hand. God was good. Even in the bad times. She'd learned that young, and the knowledge had served her well. She'd hold on to it as she tried to figure out who had been on the back porch, what he'd wanted. Not just to steal something. If that had been the case, he'd have run when she'd opened the door.

Her sweater snagged on bark, her palms stinging as slivers of wood pierced flesh. She shifted her grip, tried to find another bough to place her feet on.

Gavin grabbed her ankle, tugged gently. "Let go. I've got you."

"You've got my ankle. What good is that going to do?"

"Cassie, we don't have all night. Just trust me and let go."

Trust?

She wasn't very good at that.

"Thanks, but I can—"

"A man was murdered tonight. His killer is on the loose. How about we skip all the 'I've got to do it myself' stuff and get you down, so I can get on with my investigation?"

His words sent cold fear shooting up her spine.

The guy on her back porch had looked like he could kill someone without batting an eye or feeling a bit of remorse. Had he been looking for another victim when he'd arrived at All Our Kids?

She let go.

Gavin managed to grab her waist as she fell, lowering her to the ground with so little effort, it was almost embarrassing that she'd doubted him. After all, the guy towered over her. Six-two to her five-three, and he had muscle to spare. Obviously, he worked out. A lot. He probably also ran, biked and swam. She spent most her time chasing kids around.

"Thanks," she murmured, stepping away and nearly bumping into Gavin's huge dog. It looked like a German shepherd but was nothing like Miss Alice's old dog Angus. He'd been a shepherd, too, his muzzle already white with age by the time Cassie moved into her last foster placement. At fourteen, she'd thought she'd known just about everything, but she'd known nothing about love, commitment, respect. Miss Alice had taught her those things, and if she'd still been around, she'd have been happy to see Cassie putting them to good use.

"Sorry," she said to the dog. Its ears perked up, its dark eyes watching her every move. At least it had stopped growling, snapping and foaming at the mouth. The last part might have been more her imagination than anything.

"She forgives you," Gavin said dryly. "Now, how about you tell me what you're doing out here?"

"Running for my life. And, not from your dog. There was someone at All Our Kids tonight."

He stilled, his eyes blazing, his expression unreadable. "When?"

"Maybe ten minutes before I ran into you. He was out on the back porch."

"Doing what?"

"I have no idea. I heard him, thought he was one of the kids. I opened the door and there he was."

"Did you get a good look at his face?" He pressed a hand to her lower back, issued a command to Glory and started walking.

"Yes."

"Did you recognize him?"

"No. He was a stranger." They made it onto the path that led from All Our Kids to Harland Jeffries's mansion. An easy walk for anyone who knew the way.

An easy route for someone who might have murder on his mind.

The thought left her cold.

She'd known Harland for years, had been hired by him fresh out of college. She respected him, liked him, and believed in the things he stood for.

"You said someone was murdered tonight," she said before Gavin could ask another question.

"I'm afraid so."

"It wasn't Harland, was it?"

He hesitated, and she grabbed his arm, pulled him to a stop. "Gavin, *was it Harland*?"

"It was Michael. Harland was injured, too, but he survived."

"Was it a knife attack?" she asked, her eyes hot with tears. Michael had been a great guy. He'd spent a lot of time at All Our Kids, teaching the children to play football and basketball, bringing them treats. He had a heart of gold, and the world was going to be a lesser place without him in it.

"That's an odd question," Gavin responded quietly, urging her forward again. Just ahead, the path opened up into All Our Kids' yard. She could see the house, lights blazing from every window of the three-story building. A police car sat in the driveway, flashing blue-and-red light across the pavement. Virginia had called the police. It looked as though she'd woken all the kids, too. Either that or the arrival of the police had. "Not really," she responded as they moved across the acre of green lawn. "The guy on my back porch had a knife."

"Michael and Harland were both shot," Gavin said bluntly. "Michael died before the ambulance arrived. Harland called for help and was transported to the hospital."

"When?"

"About an hour ago."

"I didn't hear a thing." Not gunshots. Not ambulance sirens. Nothing. Then again, she'd been dead tired from nursing David through the flu, the windows were double-paned glass, the house well-constructed.

"You heard the guy on your back porch," he pointed out.

"I have an internal alarm that goes off when one of the kids is wandering around at night. Apparently, it doesn't work when sirens are screaming through the neighborhood."

He let out a bark of rough laughter, shook his head. "The house is pretty well built."

"And, I was dead tired. One of the kids had the flu this week, and we've got a toddler who hasn't been sleeping well." Juan Gomez's mother had died, and he'd been crying out for her for the past two nights. "I was dead to the world until I heard the guy on the porch."

"Do you think your assistant heard anything?"

"Not until I screamed."

"She came outside then? Did she see your assailant?" he asked.

"She didn't come outside, and I don't think she saw anything. She turned on a light, and it distracted the guy. I ran into the woods, and he followed." She shuddered.

"Do you think he was here for you?"

"If he was, I've got no idea why. He had a duffle and—" She remembered the smell of gasoline clinging to him or to the bag.

"What?" Gavin prodded as he led her up the front steps and onto the wide porch that wrapped around the sides of the house. She'd be hanging flower baskets soon. Destiny had been looking forward to that. She'd never had a yard or a garden, and being at All Our Kids was allowing her an opportunity to test out her green thumb.

It was so much easier to think about that than to think about Michael dead and Harland wounded. To think about someone shooting two of the nicest men Cassie had ever met.

"Cassie?" Gavin touched her shoulder, and she realized she was standing in front of the door, hand on the knob.

"Gasoline. When I walked outside I smelled it."

He frowned. "You're sure?"

"Positive."

"I don't like the sound of that," he muttered. "We found something at the crime scene. I think it might belong to one of your kids."

"What?" Her heart thundered in her chest, her mouth dry with fear. She didn't think she was going to like what he had to say, but she wanted him to say it, anyway.

He pulled a bag out of his coat pocket and holding it up so she could see what was inside. A blue mitten. Hand-knit. Child-size.

She knew who it belonged to.

David.

"Do you recognize it?" Gavin asked.

"Yes." She nodded. She'd seen the mittens earlier that day, tucked into David's pocket when she'd brought him to the doctor. Somehow, at some point, one of them had ended up near the crime scene.

Had one of the kids witnessed a murder?

"Whose is it?"

"David's, but he's the one who has the flu. He's been in bed all night."

"You're sure?"

"Positive. I was sleeping in a chair beside him."

"Someone had the mitten on. Whoever it was may have seen what happened at Jeffries place."

"You think that's why the guy was on the porch?"

"You said you smelled gasoline. It's possible the murderer saw the witness and came after him."

"And planned to burn the house down with all of us in it?" she asked, her voice shaking. She hated that, hated being afraid. She was, though. The kids were her responsibility. They counted on her, trusted her in a way they often hadn't been able to trust other adults. "I need to check on everyone. Make sure they're okay." She opened the door, ran inside.

Gavin said something, but she couldn't hear past the pulse of blood in her ears.

Voices carried from the kitchen. Kid voices. A man. Virginia—her voice high-pitched and shaky. From the sound of things, she was currently in full-out panic.

"We're going to keep the kids safe," Gavin said, his voice mixing with all the others.

She stopped, pivoting around to face him so quickly that he nearly walked into her. She was face to chest with him, staring at his coat and the K-9 insignia on it.

"I appreciate that," she said, stepping back so she could look into his face, into his dark blue eyes. "But when all is said and done, they're my responsibility. They're counting on me to keep them safe. Not the police. Not your K-9 team. If one of them was outside tonight and witnessed Michael's murder…" She swallowed a hard knot of grief and fear, forced herself to continue. "I haven't done my job."

"Kids do lots of things we can't control. You can't beat yourself up if one of them snuck out."

"Sure I can," she replied, shifting her gaze from Gavin to his dog, because she didn't want to keep looking into his eyes, didn't want to see the sympathy there.

"You can, but you shouldn't."

She would, anyway. That's the way things were when a person mothered kids. She didn't bother explaining, just headed toward the kitchen. Gavin followed. She didn't have to look to know it. She could hear his dog's feet padding on the wood floor, smell the scent of pine needles and outdoors.

She stepped into the kitchen, bracing herself for what she knew she'd find.

It was as chaotic as she'd imagined.

Destiny stood with her head in the open refrigerator, a bottle of chocolate milk in her hand. Little David sat bleary-eyed at the table. Rachel, Axel, Tommy and Kent huddled near the stove. Lila sat under the table,

her thumb in her mouth, a blanket pulled around her shoulders.

And then there was Virginia.

She sat next to David, eyes closed, tears streaming down her face as she hugged Juan, the toddler, close. Two police officers stood to either side of her. One held a cup of water and seemed intent on shoving it into Virginia's hand.

"She's dead," Virginia moaned. "I know she is. Dead and all of these children are just going to miss her so much. She's—"

"Standing right here, Virginia," Cassie cut in.

Virginia's eyes flew open and she jumped up, the chair nearly tipping over.

"You're alive!" she cried, rushing forward and throwing her free arm around Cassie. "I heard you scream and I thought the worst."

"I'm fine. Sorry for scaring you."

"Scaring me? You took a dozen years off my life."

"Sorry about that, too," Cassie responded.

"What happened?" Virginia asked, bouncing Juan on her hip. The poor little guy's eyes were wet from tears, his face red. He reached for Cassie, and she took him, kissing his soft cheek and murmuring the kind of comfort she figured a mother would offer.

She didn't know.

She'd never had a mother.

Just a father who'd had little use for her and a grandma who'd been too busy growing pot in her backyard and selling drugs from her living room to pay much attention to Cassie.

"Nothing that I want to discuss in front of the kids," she responded, smiling brightly at Destiny. The teen-

ager wasn't buying it. She took a sip of chocolate milk and scowled.

"Adults always have secrets. It's stupid."

"No secrets, Destiny. Just a need to have a little quiet. It's so loud in here, I can barely hear myself think," Cassie said. "Would you mind helping Virginia get everyone tucked back into bed while I speak with the police?"

"Yes," Destiny snapped. "I would mind."

But, she crouched and reached for Lila's hand, pulling her out from under the table with a gentleness that belied her angry expression.

"I'll do my best to get them settled." Virginia sighed. "But you know how things get when they're up after bedtime."

She did, and it was never good.

"Thanks, Virginia. I'll fill you in on things when you're done."

"With the way this crew is, I may never be done." She took Juan from her arms. "Come on, sweetie. Time to go back to bed. The rest of you, too. Tomorrow is Sunday, and we've got to be up early for church."

"I hate church," Destiny griped, snagging a cookie from a jar on the counter and shoving it into her mouth. A small chunk fell to the floor and landed near Glory. The dog didn't even drop her eyes. She was staring at Gavin as if the sun and moon rose and set on his command.

"I don't hate church," Tommy said with a scowl. "God is good, and church is good." At seven years old, he was way too serious for his age, years of neglect and abuse causing him to sink into himself and hide from the world.

"I'm glad you feel that way, Tommy," Cassie said gently, touching the little boy's shoulder. "Now, you go

on to bed. I'll be up in a few minutes to check under your bed."

"And in the closet, too, Cassie. That's where the bad guys like to hide the most." He looked up at her, his eyes wide and solemn.

"I'll check in your closet, too. And, in your book bag and in your church shoes."

"Bad guys can't fit in shoes," he responded, not even a hint of a smile curving his mouth.

"You're right, but I'll check, anyway. Now—" she gave him a gentle nudge toward the doorway "—go on. To bed."

He shuffled away, his dark hair falling over sea-green eyes, his flannel pajamas bagging around his narrow frame. He didn't say a lot. He'd come from a family where right words and wrong words, right actions and wrong ones all led to a harsh word, a slap, a punch or a kick. Even after seven months of living in a safe environment, he still scurried around at the edge of the action, tiptoed through the rooms to avoid being noticed, sat still as a statue while everyone else talked and giggled.

"You didn't ask any of them about the mitten," Gavin said as she filled the teapot, set it to boil. She didn't want tea, but she needed something to do with her hands.

"I know."

"I guess you have a reason for that?"

"My kids are…vulnerable. I don't want them to think they're being accused of something."

"I get it." He sighed. "More than you might imagine, but we don't have time to worry about your kids' sensitivities."

"I know, and I know you need a witness, but—"

"I want a witness," he said, cutting her off. "But I'm more concerned with keeping your kids safe."

"I'll talk to them." She crossed the room, would have walked out into the hall, but one of the officers stopped her.

"Ma'am, we'd like to ask you a few questions before you do that."

She tensed. She'd spent too many years being on the wrong side of crime-busting efforts, too many nights being pulled out of bed so the police could search her room for whatever narcotics her grandmother was suspected of selling. "About?"

"The incident on the back porch," the older of the two responded, his dark brown gaze shifting to Gavin. "Unless you're stepping in on this, Captain?"

Gavin wasn't stepping in. He wasn't leaving, either. He had questions, and someone at All Our Kids had answers. He needed to find out who. Aside from Juan Gomez, it could have been any of the children he'd seen in the kitchen.

Juan...

His mother Rosa Gomez had been Harland's housekeeper. She'd been found at the bottom of a cliff in President's Park two days ago. DC police were investigating.

Three deaths connected to the same family?

It seemed a stretch to think it was coincidence.

He'd have to bring it up to the team. First, he had to interview Cassie's kids. He understood her need to protect them, he even admired it, but he wasn't going to let it get in the way his job.

"It's all yours," he responded, his focus on Cassie.

She looked scared, but she also looked determined.

Hopefully that determination wasn't going to be a problem. He didn't want to waste time fighting her for access to the kids.

The officer nodded. Just like Dane Winthrop, Paul Anderson was someone Gavin had worked with during his days with the DC police force. Serious and hard-working, he had a reputation for following leads to the end, never giving up, never backing down. "Looks like you've got quite a bruise on your cheek," he said, and Cassie touched the swollen spot.

"Yeah. The guy with the knife wasn't real happy to see me."

"Guy with a knife?" Paul asked. "Ms. Johnson didn't mention that."

"Virginia didn't know about him," Cassie explained quickly, giving Paul the same story she'd given Gavin. That was good. Her memories seemed clear, the details she offered matching the ones she'd provided before.

When she finished, Paul opened the door that led onto the back porch. "You say you heard him?"

"I heard a thump. I thought it was one of the kids playing around." She frowned. Probably remembering that one of them had wandered to Harland's property and possibly witnessed a murder.

"Is that why you didn't call the police before you went outside?" Paul's partner asked. Young with dark hair and an almost too-pretty face, he looked like a rookie who was desperate to prove his merit. "Because it seems to me—"

"Yes." She cut him off. "That's why."

She followed Paul outside, her dark red hair spilling down her back, bits of pine needle and dead leaves sticking out of it. She was still barefoot, the cuffs of

her jeans dragging the floor, her dusty toes peeking out from under them.

"It still smells like gasoline out here," she commented.

Gavin didn't know who she was directing it at, but he doubted anyone needed it pointed out. The acrid scent stung his nose, made his eyes water.

He crouched. The fumes were thicker there, the scent so strong, he could have lit a match and caused an explosion.

"We need to get a hazmat crew out here," he said.

"You want to call that in, Shane?" Paul said to his partner. "And walk around to the front? See if there's gasoline anywhere else. Looks like someone was trying to burn the place down."

It's what Gavin had been afraid of, and he wasn't surprised to have it confirmed.

"Who would do something like that? Kill a bunch of children?" Cassie whispered, her freckles standing out against pale skin.

"Someone who would kill a well-known and well-liked attorney," he responded. "Someone who wanted to protect his identity and stay out of jail. Someone who saw a child running away from the crime scene, but likely didn't get a good enough look to know which child it was."

"You think this is connected to the murder at the congressman's place?" Paul asked.

"We found a mitten near the scene. It belongs to one of the kids who live here," he responded, scanning the empty yard. Beside him, Glory paced restlessly.

"So the guy thought he'd kill them all?" Paul shook his head. "Every time I think I've seen it all, I'm proven wrong. You got a good look at the guy?" he asked Cassie.

"Yes," she responded.

"Think you could identify him if you saw him again?"

She nodded, her face so pale, Gavin thought she might pass out.

"Maybe you should go back inside, Cassie. Get some tea, sit down," he suggested. He needed her focused and calm. Not panicked…or unconscious.

"And give the guy more time to get away? I'd rather help hunt him down."

"Your time would be better spent giving us a good description," Paul said.

"I'll take Glory out after we get you back inside," Gavin cut in.

"I'm fine," she insisted, stepping to the edge of the porch and pointing to the east. "That's the direction I ran. He wasn't far behind me. Your dog can probably—"

"Cassie," he interrupted. "I appreciate your help, but the guy could still be hanging out in the woods. If he's the same guy who shot Michael and Harland, he has a gun. It wouldn't be that hard for him to take a potshot from those trees."

"If you're trying to scare me," she said. "You've succeeded."

"All I'm trying to do is—"

"Keep me safe?" She walked inside, moving deeper into the kitchen.

He followed, wanting to remind her a dozen times that she was in danger and that she needed to play by his rules. She knew it, though. There was no sense beating her over the head with it. "Yes."

"Thanks." Cassie shivered, dropping into one of the kitchen chairs. The bruise on her cheek looked darker, her oversize pink sweater and bare feet making her look

young and vulnerable. "But, I'm pretty good at keeping myself safe." She brushed a hand over her hair, frowned as she pulled a few leaves out of the wild curls.

"Not from this kind of creep," Paul said as he stepped inside. "You saw him. He's going to want to take you out. You're going to need more than yourself to stay safe."

"I'll keep that in mind," she responded, tapping her fingers on the table. She had short nails. No polish. It looked as though she'd gotten a couple of cuts and scrapes climbing out of Glory's reach. Gavin was tempted to tell her she should wash the wounds out, put some bandages on.

"Can you give me a description of the perp?" he asked instead. He needed to get out into the woods, see if he and Glory could track the guy.

"Blond, short hair. Kind of a military cut. Not very tall. Lots of muscle, though." She shivered and Gavin shrugged out of his jacket and dropped it around her shoulders.

"I think you're going to need this more than I do," she said, but she made no move to remove it. Just scratched at a spot on the tabletop, her brow furrowed. "He was wearing black. Pants. Shirt. I'm not sure about his shoes."

"Eye color?" Paul interrupted.

"Blue. And his face..." She shook her head. "He looked dead inside."

Glory shifted, the movement subtle, her head turning toward the still-open door. Beyond it, Gavin could see the porch, the yard, a glimpse of the woods beyond.

Glory sniffed at the air, the fur on her scruff standing on end. She growled, the deep low grumbling making the room go silent.

"She see something?" Paul asked.

"Looks like it." He walked to the open door, scanned the tree line at the far edge of the property. As far as he could see, there was nothing lurking in the thick shadows there. He trusted Glory, though. The dog had good instincts, a great nose, and eyes that were a hundred times better than Gavin's.

"Better close the door after I leave and keep Cassie away from the windows," he said as he walked outside.

He waited just long enough to hear the bolt slide home before he gave Glory the command she'd been waiting for. The shepherd sprang into action, lunging off the porch and racing toward the tree line, Gavin sprinting behind her.

THREE

Gavin pulled Glory to a stop at the edge of the woods, the beam of his flashlight bobbing along dry earth. Dark trees jutted up from ground covered with a winter's worth of dead leaves. A half mile in, a small tributary meandered through the thick forest. Usually, the Royal River was nothing more than a creek that flowed across the congressman's land. The winter had been brutal, though, and melting snow had probably turned it into a rapidly flowing stream.

"Hopefully, our guy didn't have a raft or boat with him," he muttered. "If he did, we may lose the trail there."

Glory's ears perked up, but she kept her head down, nose snuffling dead leaves and earth.

She'd pick up the scent again. Gavin trusted her to do that as much as he trusted the German shepherd to do the job she'd been trained for. Not search and rescue. Protection. Together, they'd been assigned more than one case that involved protecting high-level political figures.

Tonight, they hadn't been able to protect Michael and Harland. They would find the gunman, though, and they'd protect Cassie and her kids. There was no other option. "Gavin!" someone called.

Gavin turned, caught sight of Chase Zachary hurrying toward him. Chase hadn't been working with the Capitol K-9 Unit for long, but there was no doubt he belonged. A former Secret Service agent, he worked hard and knew the ropes. His Belgian Malinois Valor knew them, too. The dog moved beside Chase, ears alert, body tense.

"Glad you're here. There's been an incident at All Our Kids," Gavin said, turning his attention back to Glory, who'd found the trail again and was moving through thick foliage and deeper into the trees.

"I heard the call come in while I was on the road searching for your perp. Adam and Brooke are still at the crime scene working with the DC police."

That was fine with Gavin. Adam Donovan and Brooke Clark would keep things flowing smoothly. Veteran members of the K-9 Unit Team, they'd have no trouble cooperating with the police.

"Good. Any sign of a vehicle on the road?"

"No vehicle. No perp. There is something, though. It was found at the crime scene."

That caught Gavin's attention, made his pulse jump. "What?"

"I saw a gold pendant about fifty feet away from where Michael's body was discovered. It looked like it had been kicked under some leaves. The thing was clean as a whistle. No dirt embedded in it. Nothing to indicate it had been lying there for any length of time."

"There's more to it than that, right?" Because Gavin knew Chase. The guy was clear thinking and had spot-on instincts. No way would he have come looking for Gavin if there wasn't something compelling about the find. "I know who the pendant belongs to."

There it was.

The missing piece to the puzzle.

Gavin met Chase's eyes. "Who?"

"Michael's girlfriend."

"Erin Eagleton? You're sure about that?" Gavin pushed through a thick stand of evergreens, the loamy scent of damp earth filling his nose. Glory was ten feet ahead, working the trail, her head down, tail up, ears alert. She'd found what she wanted, and she was going to keep chasing it until it led to the prize.

"Would I be telling you if I wasn't? It's an unusual pendant. A starfish with the initials E.E. engraved in it."

"There are plenty of people in this world with those initials."

"How many of them are dating a guy who just turned up dead?"

"We can't make assumptions, Chase. You know that. We can look for DNA on the locket, we can ask Erin if it belongs to her—"

"It's hers."

He sounded certain, so certain that Gavin wondered just exactly how he could know what kind of pendant a socialite like Erin would have hanging from her neck. She came from money and privilege and, as far as Gavin knew, didn't hang in the same circles as Chase. "I think there's a story here that you need to tell me. How about we skip all the extraneous stuff and get right to the details?"

"Erin and I are…old friends."

"As in you were dating?" He hoped not. He really did, because that would complicate things. *If* the pendant belonged to Erin and *if* they determined that she'd been at the scene when the murder occurred, a team

member who'd had a recent relationship with her might be a problem.

"A long time ago. When we were in high school."

"Okay." That wasn't as bad as he'd thought.

"I saw her tonight, though. Near the National Monument. I was working a reported mugging and ran into her there."

"You're going to tell me she was wearing that pendant, aren't you?" he asked as he picked his way down a steep incline. Glory was just ahead, stopped in her tracks, nose to the ground. She'd lost the scent, and she turned in circles, trying to catch it again.

"Yeah. I am," Chase responded. "We were in a well-lit area, and I saw it clear as day."

"What time was that?"

"Ten. A few minutes after."

"The shooting was called in at 11:30. She'd have had plenty of time to get from the National Monument to Harland's place."

"That doesn't mean she committed the crime," Chase shot back.

"No need to get defensive."

"I'm not getting defensive. I'm stating a fact. Pure and simple. She was at the mansion tonight, but that doesn't mean she pulled the trigger. If she did, Harland would have said as much."

"Maybe."

"What's that supposed to mean?"

"Harland didn't see the shooter." The congressman had been shot in the shoulder and lost plenty of blood, but he'd been lucid when the police had arrived. The first responding officer had traveled in the ambulance with him and conducted an interview on the way to the

hospital. Margaret had been given the information he'd obtained, and she'd passed it on to Gavin. No mention of anyone at the mansion except a couple of staff members and Michael. "And he didn't mention Erin being at the mansion tonight."

"She might have been visiting Michael and left before Harland saw her," Chase responded.

"Could be." One way or another, Gavin found it interesting that his coworker felt the need to defend a woman he'd dated over a decade ago. "If that pendant really is hers, we know she was there tonight. We need to find out why and when. We need to know if she saw anything, heard anything. The sooner the better."

"Want me to question her?"

"I need you out here. I'll send Brooke to her place."

Somewhere behind them, a branch snapped, the sound discordant in the midnight silence.

Both dogs alerted, their ears twitching, their tails still and straight as they shifted their gazes to the deep woods they'd just come through.

Another branch snapped.

Glory growled.

She knew what she was hearing. Not the stealthy movement of a deer. Someone was in the woods, and whoever it was seemed to be between Gavin and All Our Kids.

That didn't make him happy.

He gestured to Chase. "The suspect might be heading back to the foster home," he mouthed.

Chase nodded. "What's the plan?"

"Let's separate. Try to hem him in."

Chase nodded, taking two steps away and melting into the trees. There one minute. Gone the next.

Gavin issued a short quiet command, and Glory took off, moving through trees and foliage with unerring purpose. She had the scent. She was going to find the perpetrator, and the person who'd shot and killed Michael Jeffries was going to be made to pay for it.

Like Cassie, most of the children staying at All Our Kids didn't trust the police. They'd come from a variety of homes, foster placements and difficult situations, but the one thing they all had in common was a deep-seated distrust of authority. In her three years working as housemother, that seemed to be the one and only overriding theme, the piece of baggage every single one of her kids brought into the home. She spent a lot of time working with the kids to help them overcome that, and each child spent time with counselors and therapists.

That was all well and good, but right at that moment, it didn't matter. In the wee hours of the morning, with darkness pushing against the kitchen window and sleep still fogging their brains, there wasn't one of the seven kids who wanted anything to do with Officer Anderson.

With Virginia upstairs trying to settle Juan back down, Cassie was having to deal with the attitudes, the silences and the tears on her own.

It probably would have been a good idea if a female officer had conducted the interview. Most of the kids responded better to female authority, but Officer Anderson hadn't wanted to waste time bringing someone else in.

She'd warned him, told him it wouldn't be a waste of time if it helped open the mouths of her charges.

He'd insisted on doing things his way.

And, now they were all in the kitchen, the sharp scent of gasoline seeping in from under the back door.

The dead-eyed guy had been trying to burn the house down.

The smell was a constant reminder and a distraction. One Cassie didn't want or need. The Hazmat team would be there eventually. For now, she had to fight to keep from gagging every time she inhaled. She eyed the kids, all of them seated at the oversize table, their eyes sharp, their faces set in an array of scowls. They looked like a mutiny getting ready to happen.

"Your silence doesn't change anything. Someone," Officer Anderson said, his voice just a little too loud, "was outside of the house tonight. That person needs to own up to it." He speared each kid with a look meant to melt their defiance.

None of them even blinked.

"Confess to it," he continued. "Before you find yourself in more trouble."

"You're not in trouble," Cassie broke in, knowing full well that threatening the kids wasn't going to help. "You won't be in trouble if you admit you were outside."

Nothing.

Not a peep from anyone.

There was strength in numbers, the silence of one bolstering the silence of the others. They should have talked to each child individually, but Officer Anderson had wanted to save time. Another mistake on his part. The guy seemed kind enough, but he hadn't wanted to listen to anything Cassie had to say.

Typical, her childish self whispered. The piece of her that was still the young kid being yanked from her bed every other night, police streaming into her room and demanding that she get up, wanted to tell Officer Anderson that they were done playing twenty questions.

The more mature part, the part that wanted to keep her kids alive, the part that wanted to stay alive with them, knew she needed to keep her mouth shut and let him do his job.

"Right. Sorry. I shouldn't have said trouble. No one is in trouble," Officer Anderson agreed, his gaze jumping from one child to another. "I just need to know where you were, what you saw."

"Destiny?" Cassie prodded. She doubted the young girl would have wandered to the congressman's house, but the kid seemed to know everything about everyone in the house. If someone else had left, she'd probably know it.

"What?" Destiny asked, studying her nails like they were way more interesting than Cassie or Officer Anderson.

"Did you hear anyone leave the house tonight?"

"No."

"You're sure?"

"I was sleeping like a baby until you started screaming, and truth be told, I want to be sleeping again."

"How about everyone else?" Officer Anderson's asked. Maybe he thought he could read guilt or fear on their faces.

They just kept staring at him like he had two heads.

"Look." He raked a hand over his hair, paced to the sink and turned to face the kids again. "A blue mitten was found over near the congressman's house. One of you dropped it. You might as well 'fess up."

"I have blue mittens," David piped up. "But I wasn't wearing them tonight. They're in my coat pocket."

"Where's your coat?" Officer Anderson asked.

"I don't know."

"Son, you don't just misplace a coat. Obviously, you wore it recently. How about you think about it a little more carefully?"

David shrank back, sliding down so low in his chair, Cassie thought he might slip right under the table.

"It should be in the closet," Cassie offered. "How about you go look for it?"

David scrambled out of the chair and ran from the room. It would only take him a couple of seconds to reach the coat closet. He'd probably take longer. If he came back at all.

"These kids leave the house at night very often?" Officer Anderson asked.

More than she wanted. She'd thought about putting an alarm system in, but too many of the kids had been in homes where there were bars on the windows, security systems, guard dogs. "Occasionally."

"You ever think of putting in a security system?"

"I've thought about it."

"You might want to think on it some more. This neighborhood is safe, but that doesn't mean young kids can't get into trouble."

"I'll keep that in mind." She tried to keep the sarcasm out of her voice, but she wasn't sure she was successful. She'd spent the past three years proving that she could do her job and do it well. Harland had always believed in her, but there were plenty of other people who'd doubted. There were plenty of people who still doubted. Based on Officer Anderson's comment, she'd say he was one of them.

"You want some help with it, I can give you a hand. I have a friend in the security business. He'll put it in for free. Just cost a weekly fee for the security monitoring."

His offer stole away some of her frustration. He might be going about things in the wrong way, but his heart was in the right place. That was what counted. That was one of the things Ms. Alice had taught her. To look at the heart, to judge according to motive rather than outcome. *Everyone messes up*, she'd always say when Cassie found herself in trouble again. *But, if the heart is right, mistakes can be fixed.*

She took a deep breath, tried to smile. "I appreciate that, Officer Anderson. Once Harland recovers, I'll ask what he thinks. I usually run things by him before I make any changes to the house."

"The way I hear it, the congressman is doing well, but he might not be out the hospital for a couple of days. I'm not sure you want to wait that long."

"I—"

"Cassie." David appeared in the kitchen doorway. "My coat isn't in the closet."

"You're sure?" She'd hung it there after their trip to the doctor's office. She was certain of it. With eight kids to take care of, she couldn't afford to waste time searching for things like coats or shoes.

"I looked about sixteen times," he responded.

She wasn't sure he'd looked that many, but he was young and it was easy to miss things. "Destiny, would you mind—"

She never finished.

The window exploded, glass flying across the kitchen, kids screaming. Officer Anderson dropped to the ground, blood spurting from his shoulder or his chest. Cassie didn't know which, didn't have time to think about it. She yelled for the kids to run, then darted forward to

grab Officer Anderson by the arms. Another shot, this one whizzing past Cassie's head.

She dragged Officer Anderson out of the kitchen and into the hall, the kids' screams ringing in her ears.

"Everyone up the stairs," she shouted, her heart thundering as she dragged Officer Anderson further away from the kitchen.

He groaned but didn't open his eyes.

Something slammed into the back door.

Once. Twice. Again.

Please, God, let the kids be hiding. Please keep them safe.

"I called the police. They're on the way!" Virginia pressed in beside her, grabbing at Officer Anderson, frantic sobs coming from her throat as she helped drag him back.

The banging continued, the sound reverberating through the house. They made it to the stairs before the back door crashed open with so much force the entire house seemed to shake. Or maybe it was Cassie who was shaking, fear stealing her breath and making her heart skip frantically. She met Virginia's eyes.

"Go get the kids. Hide them until the police arrive," Cassie whispered as she pressed the hem of her sweater to a wound in Officer Anderson's right shoulder. His eyes were still closed, his body slack.

"I can't leave you here," Virginia cried, tears streaming down her face.

"You can't stay!" Cassie hissed. "Someone has got to protect the kids."

"But—"

"Go!" she mouthed.

Virginia took off running, up the stairs, out of sight.
And it was just Cassie and Officer Anderson.
And whoever had broken through the back door.

FOUR

Gavin crept around the side of the house, Glory moving silently beside him. Chase was close. Maybe a quarter mile back in the woods, running toward the house and the gunshots they'd heard. There wasn't time to wait for him.

The back door of the house had been kicked in and hung listlessly from the top hinge. He motioned for Glory to heel, then eased into the room. Glass on the floor near the sink. Pool of blood nearby. More blood in a swath that led from the sink into the hallway. His jacket lying near the table.

Glory stood facing the hall, her scruff standing on end, every muscle in her body taut. She didn't make a sound, though, and Gavin listened. No movement in the hallway. No sounds from upstairs.

Gavin unhooked Glory's lead and gave her the hand signal. She took off, nearly flying through the open doorway and into the hallway. Gavin followed, gun drawn, adrenaline pumping. A man stood near the front door. Tall. Broad. Strong. Those were Gavin's first impressions. A dark ski mask covered the guy's face, and he glared out from it, eyes icy blue as he held Cassie with one arm locked around her arms and chest, a handgun

pressed to the underside of her chin. A few feet away, Paul lay on the ground, blood spreading in a crimson stain under his back. If he lost much more, he'd die.

"You come any closer, cop," the perp said, "and I'll kill her." He jabbed the gun against Cassie's jaw to emphasize the point. She didn't flinch. Didn't panic. There were no tears, no wide-eyed pleas for help. In all the years he'd worked as a DC cop and all the years he'd been part of the Capitol K-9 team, Gavin had never seen her kind of calmness in a civilian.

"Put the gun down," Gavin responded, not moving closer, but not stepping back. He'd had training with hostage negotiation teams. Not enough to be an expert, but enough to know that he needed to make himself as unthreatening as possible.

"I don't think so," the man snarled, jabbing Cassie with the gun again. "Call off your attack dog."

Glory wasn't *on* the attack.

If she had been, the gun would have already been out of his hand. Gavin could have signaled for Glory to take the guy down, but the gun was too close to Cassie, the risk was too high.

"Let the woman go," he said instead. "Walk out the door. Leave now before things get worse for you."

"I'm not the one who needs to worry about things getting worse," the guy mocked. He was confident, and that was going to play in Gavin's favor. He'd make a mistake. Overestimated his chance at success. Gavin was ready to take advantage of that. Glory was ready, too, a constant low-level growl emanating from deep in her throat.

"You wait much longer to leave, and you'll be trapped. I've got backup coming."

The guy shrugged, but he was edging closer to the

door, his gaze on Glory. "They're not going to do any more than you are. No cop wants a civilian killed." He jabbed Cassie again.

She didn't flinch.

Didn't meet Gavin's eyes.

Was she in shock?

"And no criminal wants to die. You kill her, and that's what's going to happen."

"Right," the guy said, but the words had gotten to him. Gavin could tell by his tension, the quick darting of his gaze from Glory to the hallway beyond.

"Just let her go and—"

"Shut up and let me think! I'm the one in charge!" the man shouted. "I have her life in my hands, and you're too much of an idiot to know it!"

Glory snarled, the sound low and deep and meant to intimidate.

"*Call off your dog!* You don't, and the woman gets it first, then the mutt."

"Cease!" Gavin commanded, not because he was afraid of the threat. Glory could take the guy down in seconds. He was afraid of how much damage could be done to Cassie in those heartbeats of time it took his partner to lunge.

Glory settled onto her haunches, her dark gaze glued to the perp. She was ready. Gavin was ready.

Was Cassie?

He met her eyes. Not even a hint of terror in her dark green gaze.

"That's better," the perp muttered. "That's what I like to see. Now, you just stay here, and I'll take our friend for a little walk. I get a little away from you and that

dog, and I'll let her go. Simple and easy. Everyone will be safe. Everyone will be fine."

Except for Anderson who groaned quietly, his skin ashen.

The perp shifted, the gun pressed so deeply into Cassie's flesh, her skin bulged around the barrel. "Open the door!" he commanded.

Cassie reached for the knob, eased the door open. A screen door lay beyond, still closed, the black night pulsing behind it. There were officers out there, moving in. Gavin was certain of it. If the perp suspected anything, he didn't show it.

He kicked the storm door. "This one, too! Quick!"

Cassie moved, something in her face, something in the complete and utter stillness of her expression warning Gavin that she had no intention of walking outside.

"Cass—" he started to say, but she was already dropping, her weight breaking the perp's hold. The gun went off, the bullet barely missing her head as she fell to the floor.

"Protect!" Gavin commanded, and Glory leaped forward, teeth bared as she crashed into the perp. He fell against the storm door, and it flew open, the gun dropping from his hand and clattering onto the porch.

Glory snarled, teeth sinking into the guy's arm.

The guy let out a string of curses that would have made a sailor blush, his feet kicking at the shepherd as he tried to yank his arm out of the dog's mouth.

"The more you struggle, the harder she's going to bite," Gavin said.

"Then maybe I'll just have to make sure she can't bite anymore," the perp growled, pulling something from his pocket and jabbing it into Glory's side.

She collapsed, and Gavin's heart nearly stopped. Glory wasn't just a dog. She was family. He wanted to run to her, but protocol dictated he take down the perp before he helped his injured partner.

Gavin aimed his gun.

"Freeze!" he shouted, issuing the warning because training demanded it.

The perp yanked something from his jacket pocket tossed it onto the floor. There was a flash of light, the harsh scent of smoke. Flames licked at floor and the door frame, and Gavin fired a shot, knew he'd missed his mark.

The flames ate at the hardwood, and he stomped them out, Cassie right beside him, her breathing frantic and uneven.

It only took seconds to put out the small fire, seconds to run out onto the porch. The perp had disappeared around the side of the house or into the tree line. Gavin flashed his light into the shadows, searching for movement, some clue as to which direction the perp had gone.

"Gavin!" Chase called as he sprinted around the corner of the house, Valor loping beside him. "I heard another gunshot. Everyone okay?"

"Glory's down. One DC officer down. Call for an ambulance and the vet," he responded as he flashed his light into the darkness, praying that he'd catch a glimpse of the intruder.

Nothing. Not even a whisper of movement in the trees. The guy was close, though. He had to be. Gavin took off across the yard, running toward the trees, his gut telling him that the perp had headed there.

Sirens screamed and two police cruisers raced into view. Both DC police. One of them a K-9 unit. Good.

They needed more officers and dogs on the ground. And Gavin needed Glory. They were a team. Tracking a suspect without her felt odd and a little disorienting. He'd do it, though. He'd put everything, every fear for his partner, every worry aside to get the job done.

"You have any idea which way the perp headed?" Chase asked, jogging up beside him, Valor sniffing at the ground and then the air, his ears perked, his tail still.

"I'd guess he went into the woods. No way would he head toward the road. Not with police everywhere. If he'd gone toward the back of the house, Valor would have heard him."

Chase nodded. "You want me to take Valor in to look for him while you fill the DC guys in?"

What Gavin really wanted to do was go into the woods himself, hunt the guy down. But he'd been at the scene, spoken to the perp, looked in the guy's eyes.

"Yes," he responded reluctantly. "Radio in if you find anything."

"Will do!" Chase raced away, Valor loping along beside him.

Gavin jogged back to the house. Three officers were inside, two hovering over Cassie as she pressed what looked like a dish towel to Paul's shoulder.

The third was beside Glory, murmuring something to the dog that Gavin couldn't hear. Glory's tail thumped, and she managed to get onto her feet, her gait a little stiff as she walked to Gavin's side. No blood that he could see. No evidence of a knife wound.

He frowned, touching what looked like singed hair on her flank.

"Looks like a Taser," one of the officers said. Young with gaunt face and a narrow frame, he looked like a high

school kid. He was right, though. It seemed as though Glory had been Tased.

If that was the case, she'd recover well.

Relief coursed through him, and he scratched behind her ears, looked into her eyes. "Good job, Glory," he said, offering the praise she craved.

In their three years working together, Glory had never been injured, never been ill, never missed a day of work. She loved her job, and even now, she seemed excited, her tail wagging, her eyes bright.

Paul, on the other hand, had lost every bit of his color. Gavin knelt beside him, nudging in close to Cassie, feeling the corded muscles of her shoulder and arm as he set his hand over hers, added more pressure to the wound.

"How far out is the ambulance?" he asked, glancing at one of the officers, wondering if he could apply enough pressure to staunch the blood. Wondering if it was too late for that to do any good.

"Should be coming up the driveway now."

"Someone needs to bring them in. We're on limited time."

"Not that limited," Paul murmured, his eyes still closed. "I got a fifteenth wedding anniversary coming up. I die, and my wife will kill me."

If the situation hadn't been so dire, Gavin would have laughed. "You've got big plans for your anniversary?" he asked. He needed to keep Anderson conscious and talking.

"Cruising to the Bahamas. Wife's been planning this trip for years. If I don't make it, she'll kill me." He opened his eyes, offered a smile that was more a grimace. "Also, I got a score to settle with someone, and I'm not going anywhere until I settle it."

"You're not going anywhere, period," Cassie cut in, her tone brusque and matter-of-fact. Her hand was steady beneath Gavin's, her expression calm. "Except the hospital. Where they'll fix you up and get you ready for that big anniversary trip."

"Right," Paul rasped. Gavin wasn't sure he believed Cassie's words, but he was putting on a good show, making an effort to stay conscious.

Gavin had seen people live through worse injuries. He'd seen them die with lesser ones. God was in control of the outcome. Not willpower. Not medical intervention. It had taken a long time for Gavin to believe that, to accept it.

An ambulance crew hurried in, and Gavin put a hand on Cassie's elbow, helping her to her feet as the medical team moved in and began to stabilize Paul.

A living room opened out to the left of the foyer, and he brought her there, waiting as the crew stabilized Paul and lifted him onto the gurney.

"I'll ride along with them," one of the DC police officers offered.

Good. Gavin didn't want Paul to be alone, but he wasn't willing to leave Cassie and the kids. The perp hadn't been playing games, and he hadn't intended for Cassie to survive.

Gavin met her eyes, saw the fear she'd been keeping at bay.

"You okay?" he asked, and she nodded, her gaze skittering away.

"Fine." She shrugged away from his hold, marched through the living room and into the kitchen. The place looked like a war zone—broken window, blood, shards of glass and bits of wood.

"This is a crime scene, Cassie. You need to stay out until we can process it," Gavin said because it was true, and because he didn't want Cassie anywhere near the broken window or door

"Can I wash my hands?" She held them up. They were covered in blood and shaking. A lot.

"How about you do it in the bathroom upstairs?" He took her arm, felt her muscles trembling as he turned her around and guided her back into the hall. It wasn't much better in there. Blood on the floor, door open, soot staining the walls and floor.

Officers were there, processing the scene and collecting evidence, but he kept himself between Cassie and the door as they walked to the stairs. The perp was bold, and he had plenty to lose. No way was Gavin going to give him another shot at Cassie.

She didn't look at him and didn't speak.

He let her have her silence.

They'd have to talk eventually, but he'd give her time to clean up, get her thoughts and emotions together. It was obvious she needed to do both. She was visibly shaking, her teeth chattering as she walked up the first three steps. She reached the fourth and swayed, grabbing the railing with blood-stained hands.

He touched her back, steadying her. "Want to sit down for a minute?"

"I'm fine."

"You look a little shaky."

"I am, but I'm not going to fall on my face or tumble down the stairs and break my neck. The kids need me."

"It's okay to be upset, Cassie," he said.

"I didn't think I needed permission, but thanks."

"Your sarcasm is charming," he responded. The

best thing he could offer her was something to focus on besides the blood on her hands and on her shirt, the bruise on her cheek, the memory of whatever she'd been through before he'd arrived.

"Thanks for trying," she said, glancing over her shoulder and offering a wan smile. "But a sparring match isn't going to distract me. Not when I can smell the blood on my hands. Not when I can still hear the glass shattering, see Officer Anderson falling."

"You'll feel better once you get cleaned up," he said, and she shook her head.

"No. I won't. I'm not going to feel better until I hear that Officer Anderson is going to be okay." She reached the top of the stairs, paused outside the bathroom. "But, I'm going to get cleaned up, anyway. I told Virginia to tell the kids everything was okay and keep them in their rooms. I don't want any of them to see me like this." She plucked at her shirt and frowned.

"Good idea. We don't want them any more scared than they already are," he responded, knowing that she was more concerned about that then about herself and the trauma she'd been through.

"Exactly." She stepped into the bathroom, flicked on the light. She didn't turn on the water. Just stood staring at the chipped sink as if she didn't quite know what she was supposed to do there.

He reached past her, turned on the water. "There you go. Wash up."

"Sorry. Thanks." She grabbed soap, shoved her hands under the water.

He waited, his gaze dropping to the little chip in the white porcelain. He knew how it had gotten there. Knew how long it had taken to hang the oversize mirror on the

wall, how many tiles it had taken to finish the floor. He'd
helped Harland do both the year he'd turned sixteen. Part
of his restitution for stealing the congressman's wallet.
That was how they'd met. Gavin, a brash and angry fos-
ter kid who'd barely qualified for his Junior class trip
to DC, and Harland, a veteran congressman who liked
to eat lunch near the Washington Monument, sitting on
a bench and enjoying the spring weather. Gavin had
seen the wallet hanging out of Harland's back pocket
as he walked by with his class, and he hadn't been able
to resist.

He'd grabbed it, had about two seconds to celebrate
the victory before Harland snagged the back of his shirt
and told him to give it back.

He pushed aside the memory, forced himself back to
the present. Cassie seemed intent on scrubbing every bit
of skin off her palms.

"I think your hands are clean."

She frowned, staring at her scrubbed hands. "They
don't feel clean."

"That might take a little longer," he responded gently,
turning off the water, offering her the hand towel that
hung from the little rack he'd installed.

"Thanks." She smiled. A real smile. A sweet one,
and he found himself looking at her. Really seeing her.
The long red lashes and deep green eyes. The freckles
on her cheeks and nose. She was a beautiful woman. No
doubt about that. She was also his key witness, and he
had to keep her alive, keep her talking, keep her remem-
bering everything she'd seen. "Gavin! You upstairs?"
someone called.

Gavin knew the voice. He'd been working with Adam
Donovan long enough to recognize it. The guy had a

keen ability to separate important details from extraneous. He and his Doberman, Ace, were well known for their success in tracking criminals.

"Right here." He walked to the top of the stairs, Glory padding along beside him. She seemed okay. Better than okay. She seemed back to normal. Being Tased didn't seem to have done any long-term damage.

"Glory okay? I heard a call went out for the vet."

"She's good. I'm going to have the vet take a look at her, and I'm not working her for a while, but she seems to be fully recovered."

"You want me to go out and find your guy?"

"Chase is already out with Valor, and there's at least one DC K-9 team with them. It might be better if you help with evidence collection. We've got a lot of information to sort through and several crimes. A murder. Two shootings. A potential attempt at arson."

"I saw the hazmat team as I arrived," Adam said. "You call them in?"

"We've got an accelerant on the back porch. I thought it best if they take care of it."

Adam nodded. "You think there's a connection between what happened tonight and the body that was found at President's Park? The woman was Harland Jeffries's maid."

"I don't know, but I think we need to look into it."

"Are you talking about Rosa Gomez?" Cassie walked out of the bathroom. She must have splashed water on her face. The edges of her hair were damp, a few tendrils curling along the line of her jaw.

"That's right." Adam smiled, but his gaze was sharp. He was as good at questioning witnesses and victims as he was at tracking criminals. "Did you know her?"

"Yes. She used to bring her son over every few days. She helped with some of the cleaning, and the kids and I watched Juan."

"He's here now, isn't he?" Adam asked.

He knew the answer.

It was common knowledge that two-year-old Juan was staying at All Our Kids until his mother's family could be located. Since no father was listed on the birth certificate, relatives of Rosa's were the only option for giving him permanency outside of the foster system.

"Yes. We're just an interim placement for him. CPS is trying to locate extended family. If they're able to do that, it will be the best place for Juan."

"I'm sure it would be," Adam agreed. "You ever have any long talks with Rosa? She ever mention who her son's father was?"

Subtle, Gavin wanted to say.

He kept his mouth shut, waited for Cassie's answer.

"No. She never talked about anything personal." Cassie brushed a strand of hair from her cheek, her fingers trembling slightly. "Is there some reason why you think her death is connected to what happened tonight?"

"Yeah," Adam responded. "I don't believe in coincidence. Two people connected to the congressman are killed in less than three days. It's a stretch to think the deaths aren't related."

"I thought Rosa's death was an accident." Cassie frowned.

Gavin cut into the conversation. "It might have been."

The fact was, Rosa's death hadn't been ruled an accident by anyone but the media. Congressman Jeffries's housekeeper had been found at the bottom of a cliff, her purse and wallet missing, her cell phone gone. Police

suspected foul play, but in the absence of physical evidence and witnesses, they couldn't prove it. They were digging hard, trying to find a suspect and motive, but so far, they'd come up empty.

"Which means it might not have been," she added. "So, how about you explain why you think her death might have been murder."

"How about we just concentrate on figuring out what happened tonight?" Gavin tried to reroute the conversation, get it back to where he wanted to be.

"How about I go downstairs and see if the DC team has come up with anything useful?" Adam said dryly. "Then, I'll head back to the congressman's house. Brooke left for…" He glanced at Cassie, frowned. "The potential witness's house an hour ago. She should be calling in soon."

Good. Gavin was anxious to hear what Erin had to say about her visit to the Jeffries mansion. "Sounds good. I'll want an in-person update from her once she's spoken to the witness. How about we meet at headquarters in a couple of hours?"

"You want the entire team?"

"Everyone who's not on duty."

"Will do." He walked away, and Gavin turned his attention back to Cassie.

"I need to interview you, and then I'll need to talk to the kids."

"The kids—"

"A man is dead," Gavin cut in. "Two more have been injured. I think that's a good reason to ask a few more questions. I'll start with you. Then, I'll need to speak with everyone else. One at a time."

"Fine," she conceded. "We can talk in my office. It's upstairs."

* * *

She was going to puke.

She really was.

Cassie only hoped Gavin wasn't around when she did it.

She swallowed down bile, caught another whiff of blood.

Gagged.

Officer Anderson had almost died.

His blood had been gushing over her hands, and there'd been absolutely nothing she could do but apply pressure and pray.

Please, God, let him live.

She'd chanted that over and over as she'd waited for help, was still chanting it, because she believed that God would hear, that He would act. She hoped He would.

"You okay?" Gavin asked. He smelled like the outdoors—clean and fresh with just a hint of earth and rain mixed in.

That was so much better than the scent of blood which seemed to cling to Cassie's skin. She swallowed hard, trying to keep the little bit she'd had for dinner in her stomach. "I will be."

"If you need some time to get out of those clothes or—"

"No. I don't want to waste time. I'll change after I answer your questions." She broke in, because there weren't many things that could make her cry. Not sad kids. Not sad movies. Not her own grief or past sorrows. Kindness though? That got to her faster than just about anything. And Gavin? He had that look on his face. The one people wore when they felt pity or sympathy or compassion.

"It will take you two minutes to change."

"Two minutes that you don't have. You were right. A man is dead. Two men were injured."

And then there was Rosa.

Like everyone else, Cassie had believed what the media reported—a tragic accident, a fall that had led to a young mother's death.

Had Rosa been murdered?

The thought had never occurred to Cassie. Rosa had always been kind and sweet. She had obviously loved her son, obviously enjoyed her job. She'd never said much about her family. Never mentioned parents, boyfriend, husband. Cassie had her own secrets. Things that she didn't tell anyone about her past, where she'd come from and why she'd become the woman she was. So she hadn't asked anything more than what Rosa was willing to tell.

Maybe she should have. Maybe pressing for details would have saved Rosa's life or helped the police find her killer.

Cassie jogged up the stairs and hurried down the narrow hall. The third floor wasn't nearly as open and airy as the two lower floors. Harland had designed the house to serve as a home for at-risk kids, children who'd worked their way through so many foster placements that they'd have ended up in group homes or juvenile detention. They were the hard-case kids, the ones who social workers worried about, lost sleep over.

The ones Cassie loved, because she'd been one of them…until she'd walked into Miss Alice's home.

The upstairs contained two offices and two bedrooms for respite foster care, a storage room and a small library that Cassie used when one of the kids needed a time-out.

She opened the door to her office. It was the only space in the house that was just hers. No kids allowed.

She had paperwork in there, files—locked up in a cabinet—containing information about each child. She also had a computer, a small mahogany desk that Harland had bought her for Christmas two years ago and a couple of chairs. Three shelves of books that she'd been meaning to read. Most were educational. A few were fiction.

She took a seat behind the desk and smoothed her hand over a thin layer of dust. She hadn't been in the office since David's illness. Not that she ever spent much time there. Her life was too hectic to do much more than file papers.

"You want to know about the mitten," she commented as Gavin took the chair across from her, Glory dropping down on the floor beside him. The dog was bigger than most of the shepherds Cassie had seen. It was also more muscular, its coat thick and glossy.

The dog huffed, its dark eyes focused on her face, and she thought it might actually be smiling at her.

"That's right." Gavin touched Glory's head, and the dog settled onto her stomach, her head resting on her paws. "You said David had a pair and that you'd seen them earlier today. Were you and Officer Anderson able to figure out which kid had them on tonight?"

"We were trying to find David's coat when Officer Anderson was shot. The mittens were in the pocket."

"Trying? You couldn't find it?" He leaned forward, his palms resting on the table. He had the bluest eyes she'd ever seen. Not green-blue or gray-blue. Not denim. They were the clear crisp blue of the purest summer sky.

"I never made it to the coat closet. That's where it was supposed to be. David looked, but you know how kids are."

"You'd probably know more about that than I would."

He smiled, and she forgot for a moment that he was a police officer. He just looked like a man. A nice one. One that she'd have probably wanted to know more about.

If she weren't completely done with men and relationships.

She glanced away and tried to focus on the wall, the bookshelves, anything but Gavin. "Eight-year-olds aren't all that good at finding things. Even when those things are right in front of their faces."

"Would you mind if I check the closet?"

"I'll do it." She stood, because seeing that smile had made her more uncomfortable than she wanted to be.

"Cassie," he said, blocking the path between the desk and the door. "You've been attacked twice tonight. How about you stay put for a while?"

"There are police all over the place," she argued.

"And there are guns that can hit a target at 400 yards."

He had a point. One that she hadn't considered.

"The closet is——"

"I know where it is."

"I forgot. You've been here before."

"Not just been here, Cassie. I lived here for two years. I know the coat closet, the offices, the little attic space that you can only access through the storage room." He shrugged. "I'll be back in a minute. Try to relax. Take a few deep breaths. Want some water while I'm down there?"

She shook her head, because there were a dozen questions spinning through her head, a dozen things she wanted to ask about the two years he'd spent at All Our Kids, about his life before he'd become the man he was.

He walked out the door before she could.

Which was exactly what she wanted him to do.

She didn't want to think of him as anything more than a police officer. She didn't want to imagine him as a young boy without a home, a teenager without a family. She didn't want to think that he'd once been like one of her kids.

Like her.

She'd spent an entire year getting used to being single after being part of a couple. She'd spent a little more time than that wondering if taking a job as housemother was worth giving up the dreams she'd built with Kane. She'd had no choice. He'd made it really clear that she couldn't do both, and she'd felt called to the job the same way she'd felt called on a mission trip to Africa when she was in college.

She'd tried to explain it, but he'd wanted all of her attention, her time, her love or none of it.

She sighed, and Glory lifted her head, staring at Cassie with what could have been sadness.

"It's a stupid thing to be thinking about, Glory," she explained, and the dog dropped her head back onto her paws, closing her eyes. She was tired after a hard night's work.

Cassie was tired, too, but she wasn't sorry.

Not for the choice she'd made, not for the sacrifices, not for the life she'd carved out for herself and her kids. She loved her life. She didn't want it to change, but lately she'd been feeling anxious, antsy.

She'd change clothes and check on the kids while Gavin got the coat. That would keep her occupied.

She started toward the door, but Glory lumbered up, settled herself at Cassie's feet.

"I need to get by," she said, but Glory didn't move.

Cassie stepped to the side. Glory followed.

Obviously, the dog was trying to keep her in the office.

It was just as obvious, she was going to succeed, because Cassie had seen her snarling and angry, and she wasn't going to rile her up.

She settled back into her seat. Glory settled down beside it, resting her big head on giant-size paws.

Footsteps tapped on the steps, and Glory raised her head, looked at the door, her tail thumping happily. Gavin was returning, and Cassie had the horrible feeling that he was bringing change with him, that everything she'd worked for was about to disappear.

She wanted to race down the stairs, get all the kids and Virginia and run as far and as fast as she could.

There was nowhere to go, though.

So she sat and waited as the footsteps drew closer, Glory's tail thumped a little faster, and the churning ache in her stomach intensified.

FIVE

They'd been searching for an hour, and Gavin's mind was ticking off every minute of it. Nothing in the coat closet. Nothing in any of the kids' rooms. Nothing in Cassie's room or in the room of her assistant Virginia.

They finished searching the second level of the house, then searched the lower level where police officers were still processing the scene.

Nothing.

"I don't understand this," Cassie said, twirling a few strands of hair between her fingers as she opened the trash can in the kitchen. She'd changed out of her bloody clothes and into faded jeans and a black T-shirt and pulled her hair into ponytail that brushed the middle of her back. "A coat doesn't just disappear."

"It does if someone wears it outside and leaves it there," he responded. He'd thought about using Glory to find the coat, but there were so many scents in the house, so many people traipsing through that any scent trail had been diluted long ago. For a dog like Glory, that wasn't an ideal tracking situation.

"The kids know the value of a dollar. They wouldn't just leave a coat outside."

"The mitten was left outside," he pointed out.

"Accidentally." She released the strands of hair, and they sprang into a curl that bounced against her jaw. "That's what you're thinking, right? That one of them was outside, saw what happened at Harland's place, got scared and ran?"

"It's the most likely scenario."

"I know," she admitted as she opened the pantry and glanced inside. "I wish I didn't. I'd prefer to think that the kids are all safe here."

"They will be."

"You can't guarantee that, Gavin. Look what happened tonight. There was a police officer here, and someone still managed to get in."

"Trust me. Capitol K-9 can keep you safe, and we will."

"I hope so," she responded.

She closed the pantry door, then brushed what looked like flour off her jeans. "But I'm thinking that my best plan is to pack up the van and head out of town."

"Will CPS let you do that?" he asked, knowing she needed special permission to do it.

"I'm not sure that I care."

"Of course you do."

She sighed. "You're right. I guess I can put in a security system."

"Glory is a built-in security system."

"Are you suggesting I get a dog?" She crossed the kitchen, walked out into the hall. "I think we should look on the third floor. The kids usually don't go up there, but we've searched everywhere else."

"Sounds good, and I'm not suggesting anything. I'm telling you how it's going to be."

"What are you talking about?" She turned, pausing

three steps up. They were eye to eye, and he could see flecks of gold in her irises, see the edges of the bruise that seemed to be deepening with every minute that passed.

"You need to ice that." He touched the spot, and she flinched. He wasn't sure if it was from pain or surprise.

"Are you trying to change the subject?"

"Just making an observation."

"Observation noted." She started back up the stairs. "So how about you answer my question? How, exactly, are things going to be?"

"You and the kids are going to have twenty-four hour protection until we find the guy who was here tonight."

"You can't be serious." She reached the second floor and headed up to the next level.

"I told you Capitol K-9 would keep you all safe. I meant it."

"I know, and I'm all about being safe. But…"

"What?"

"I can't believe your department would want to spend the money on twenty-four hour protection." She bypassed her office, heading to the end of the hall. The storage room was there. Gavin had spent a lot of time in that room as a teen, going through boxes, looking at things left behind by other kids.

"Can you think of anything more worthy of our resources?" he asked as he walked into the large room. It looked nearly the same as it had when he was a teen, boxes stacked up against the walls, a few pieces of furniture cluttering the area.

"*I* can't, but I figured your boss might be able to." She shimmied between a love seat and a coffee table, frowned. "Just what I thought."

"You found the coat?"

"I found Destiny's stockpile of food." She lifted several apples and two juice boxes from the floor.

"We need the coat."

"I was hoping that would be here, too. A couple of the kids like to hide stuff up here. I guess they think it will be safer than their rooms. We can check the library, too. I use it for time-outs, but sometimes the kids spend time there when they want to be alone."

"That's what you're calling it now?"

"Calling what?" She led the way to a room sandwiched between the offices.

"The library. When I lived here, it was the consequence room." He'd never had to spend much time there. He'd been too thankful to be in a home, too happy to have a safe place to sleep, food in his stomach and an adult who cared.

"You mentioned that before."

"That I lived here? It's not a secret." It also wasn't something that he shared often. He'd shared the information with Cassie, because he wanted to create a bond, bridge the gap of her distrust and, hopefully, encourage her to open up a little.

"Is that why you volunteer at All Our Kids every time we have a work day?"

"One of the reasons."

"What are the others?"

"Those," he said as she walked into the library and flicked on a light, "are a secret."

"A man of mystery, huh?"

"No mystery," he replied. "I'm just a man who keeps some things close to the cuff."

She cocked her head to the side. "I see."

"What?" he asked, more curious than he wanted to be. More curious than he probably should be.

"You suffer from the same disease as my kids."

"What's that?"

"Distrust."

"I'd say that your kids and I aren't the only ones who suffer from it," he pointed out. "You haven't been all that enthusiastic about working with me."

"It has nothing to do with working with you, Gavin. I just have a thing about sharing information with people." She shrugged, stepping away from the door so that he could move into the room.

"I rest my case," he responded as he walked past her. The room was smaller than he remembered, the lone window looking out over the backyard. Bookshelves stood against each wall. Three beanbag chairs sat in the center of the floor, multicolored and well-worn. No pictures on the walls, but the space still managed to look comfortable and inviting.

"All right." She laughed nervously. "You win. Now, how about we get back to what we're here for?"

She gestured to a bright yellow beanbag chair that was half-covered with a pile of black fabric. "Looks like we've found the missing coat."

He lifted the fabric, looked at the puffy black coat. "This is David's?"

"It is." She didn't take the coat, just found one of the pockets and then the other, her hand brushing his arm, her hair brushing his chin. They were so close he could feel the heat of her body, feel the tension in her muscles. She was acting relaxed, but she was nervous, edgy. She dug deeper into the second pocket, pulled out a blue mitten and held it up triumphantly. "Success! Finally!"

"We can't call it a success until we find out who was wearing this tonight," he pointed out, and she scowled.

"You want some advice, Gavin?" she asked, lifting the hem of the coat and pulling a bit of down stuffing from a tear she found there.

"I'm not sure," he admitted. The last time he'd gotten advice from a woman, it had been screamed at him in the parking lot of his apartment building at three in the morning. Helena hadn't been pleased that he'd missed her birthday dinner, and she'd been more than happy to let everyone in the neighborhood know it.

"You do," she insisted. "So, I'm going to give it to you. Next time, allow a girl some time to celebrate her success before you go and shoot her down."

"I'll keep that in mind," he assured her, amused by her comment and by the hint of laughter in her eyes.

"Good." She fingered the tear. "This wasn't here when David wore the coat earlier today. I guess whoever wore it was hoping it wouldn't be found for a while. He probably thought the weather would warm up, and the evidence of his midnight romp through the woods wouldn't be noticed for months."

"You're assuming it was a boy."

"Destiny is too big for the coat. Rachel is afraid of the dark, and there's no way she'd have gone outside at night. Lila would have been dragging the hem. Since the hem is torn, but not dirty, I'd say she wasn't the one wearing it. The kid who took it was definitely a boy." She dropped onto a pink beanbag chair, stretched her legs out in front of her. "And he is definitely in trouble."

"For ripping the coat or for leaving the house?"

He expected her to say both, but she shook her head. "I'm not worried about the transgressions, Gavin. I'm

worried about what he saw and who might have seen him. I can't let anything happen to these kids. They've already been through so much."

"Nothing is going to happen to them. We'll find out who went outside, what he saw, and we'll find our suspect."

"It may not be that easy." She pulled her knees to her chest, wrapping her arms around them. She could have passed for one of the kids, her dark red ponytail wild and curly, the knees of her jeans torn. "These kids aren't your average kids. They've been hurt by so many people that they think that's all life has to offer. They have walls and boundaries and a million coping mechanisms."

"I know," he said simply, because he did. He'd been a kid just like that. He knew all about hurts so deep they felt like they'd never heal. He knew about being betrayed by people who should have been trustworthy. He knew about walls built so thick and so tall that it seemed impossible to tear them down.

"That's what everyone says. Until they have to deal with one of my kids." She sighed, pushed herself up from the beanbag chair and nearly toppled sideways as she tried to right herself.

He grabbed her waist, holding her steady as she caught her balance. He felt warm flesh beneath soft cotton, felt the quiet hitch of her breath.

"Oops!" she murmured, stepping away, her cheeks bright red. "Sorry about that."

"About what?"

"Nearly taking us both down."

"You weren't even close to doing that."

"Right. Okay." She turned, strode toward the door. "I'll go get Tommy."

"Is he top on the list of suspects?" he asked before she could disappear from view.

She stopped and stood for a moment without saying a word. She was uncomfortable with Gavin. He sensed the undercurrent of that in the air. He thought it was because he was a police officer, but he didn't ask. Whatever her reasons, she was going to have to deal with them. Until the perp was brought in, they'd be spending a lot of time together.

"I think," she finally said, "that a suspect is someone who might have committed a crime. Tommy isn't a criminal. He's a good kid who makes some really bad choices. If I were going to choose one out of the seven who'd have taken someone else's coat and gone on a midnight jaunt, I'd choose him. That doesn't mean he did it. It just means that he's proven he's more than capable of it. I'll bring him to my office. If you want to wait for us there, that would be great."

He'd been dismissed, and he didn't like it.

Too bad what he liked or didn't had no bearing on his job. He had a goal and a mission. Harland deserved better than unanswered questions. He deserved justice for himself and for his son. Cassie might be uncomfortable with Gavin, her kids might have walls built up to the heavens, but Gavin wasn't going anywhere until he had the information he needed. He wasn't backing down until he had what he wanted.

It was the way he worked. It was why he was good at what he did. And, it was why he had absolute confidence that they'd find the murderer. Eventually.

The kids weren't cooperating.

Cassie didn't have to be a genius to figure that out.

Tommy had been mute, not answering any of Gavin's questions except with vigorous head shakes. Destiny had been sarcastic. Kent and Axel had talked a mile a minute about nothing and everything. Blocks. Legos. School. They'd led Gavin on a merry chase, going down one conversational tangent after another.

To his credit, he'd been patient, kind, even a little amused. Now, he looked tired, the shadow of a beard staining his jaw as he listened to Rachel describe the bad man with the gun who'd tried to kill Cassie.

It was one of the best tall tales Cassie had ever heard Rachel tell.

"Rachel, you were upstairs when that happened," she reminded her gently, because it never did any good to be hard on Rachel. She'd learned to lie to cover abuse and to keep herself from being abused more. It would take a lot more than the six months Rachel had been with Cassie for that habit to be broken.

Rachel frowned, her cheeks going bright red. "I forgot."

"It's okay." Gavin smiled, and Rachel's big brown eyes widened. Cassie could almost see the stars dancing in them. "What I'm really wondering," he continued, "is whether or not you heard anything before that bad guy came in your house? Maybe a lot earlier. Before Cassie screamed and the police came?"

"Well..." Her eyes shifted to the side, and Cassie's heart jumped. No doubt about it, that was the right question to ask. There was also no doubt that Rachel *had* heard something. Whether or not they could get the information out of her remained to be seen. "I... Maybe. I don't remember."

"Are you afraid?" Gavin asked, reaching across the

table and touching Rachel's hand. It was such a sweet gesture, so unexpected in a gruff police officer, that Cassie found herself studying his face, trying to find some hint of who he really was.

He met Cassie's eyes and smiled. "Maybe you could tell her that there's nothing to be afraid of. That telling the truth always pays off, and no matter what she says, she's not going to be punished."

She could. She would. She just needed to stop staring into his eyes and focus. She broke eye contact to kneel beside Rachel. "Sweetie, it's okay. Whatever you have to say, you're not going to be in trouble. What did you hear?"

"One of the boys," she whispered, her gaze darting to the door. "I heard him leave the room and go downstairs."

"Do you know what time it was?" Gavin asked quietly.

She shook her head. "I just know it was after we were supposed to be asleep. I…was reading with my flashlight, and Destiny was snoring and so was Lila. I heard a door open and, I heard someone walking downstairs."

"It might have been Virginia," Cassie pointed out. "Or me getting David's medicine."

"No." Rachel shook her head. "It was one of the boys."

"How do you know?" Cassie asked, and Rachel fiddled with the hem of her nightgown, avoiding looking in Cassie's eyes. Another lie was coming. No doubt about it.

"I think I heard him talk."

"Who was he talking to?" Gavin asked. "Was someone else with him?"

"He was by himself. Maybe he was just talking to the wall like Cassie does."

Gavin laughed, and Rachel smiled.

Cassie wasn't amused. Rachel's story wasn't adding up, but she was too tired to figure out which parts of it were true and which were lies. "Rachel—"

"I think I have all I need for now," Gavin interrupted, his smile gentle, his expression soft. He seemed to have an affinity for the kids. That surprised Cassie. He'd been at the house quite a few times, but she'd never seen him interact with any of the children. Maybe she just hadn't noticed, because she hadn't wanted to.

Kane had been it. The One. Prince Charming and happily-ever-after tied up in a nice little package.

That's what she'd thought, because she was apparently not nearly as savvy about men as she was about kids.

When Kane had given her the ultimatum, he'd broken her heart.

She had promised herself that it would never be broken again.

That meant pouring herself into her job and ignoring the men who walked in and out of her life.

"You can go back to bed, Rachel. Maybe we can talk again tomorrow, okay?" Gavin said.

Rachel nodded and scurried out of the room.

Her feet pounded on the stairs, and a door slammed.

"She's lying," Gavin said quietly.

"I know."

"Do you have any idea why?"

"I have a dozen ideas, but until she admits it, they're not going to do us any good."

"What are your thoughts?"

"She was somewhere she shouldn't be and saw one of the boys leaving."

"Do you think you can get her to tell the truth?"

"I can try, but Rachel came from a very abusive home. She lied to stay safe."

"Poor kid," he said, and she thought he really meant it. "I've got a meeting at headquarters. I'll be back in a few hours. We'll try again then." He stood, murmuring a few words to Glory who followed him to the door.

Cassie stayed where she was. *We* made it sound as though they were a team, and she didn't want to play into that thought any more than necessary.

Gavin paused outside the door. Even with a five-o'clock shadow on his face and a layer of dirt on his clothes, he looked good. And *that* was something she shouldn't be noticing.

"I'm going to leave Glory downstairs. She'll be on guard duty until I get back," he said. "I've also got a female officer waiting outside. She'll come in when I leave and stay until I return. We're going to make sure you and the kids stay safe."

"I appreciate that."

"Hopefully when I get back, we'll be able to get a little more information out of the kids. One of them saw something, and until we find out who, all of them are in danger."

"I know."

"Good. Just make sure you don't forget that you're in danger, too. You saw the perp's face. He knows it. Stay inside, Cassie. Stay away from the windows and doors. Play it safe, because these kids need you. And the guy who killed Michael? He couldn't care less about that."

He strode away, the words seeming to echo through Cassie's head.

She knew he was right, but she didn't like it.

She wanted to turn the clock back, make sure that

none of the kids snuck outside, keep all of them safe and secure the way she always had.

She couldn't, of course.

That was the problem with life. You could only move forward. There was no way to go back and change anything.

Sometimes she dwelled on that more than she wanted to. Sometimes, she lay in bed thinking about all the things that she should have done differently.

It didn't do any good.

It wouldn't do any good this time, either.

God had a plan. He always did.

She'd just have to trust that whatever came, He'd work that plan out.

She rubbed the tension from the back of her neck, flicked off the light and headed to her bedroom. She needed a shower, needed to wash the scent of blood from her skin, wash it from her clothes. Mostly she just needed to believe that things were going to be okay. That was the hard part, because things hadn't always been okay. Just like her kids, she'd lived through a lot of tough times. She knew how quickly good could turn bad. She'd had three years of fulfilling work at All Our Kids. That didn't mean she'd have tomorrow.

An image of the gunman flashed through her head, mixing with the image of the man who'd been on the back porch. They were the same. There was no doubt about that. She'd looked into cold blue eyes, and she'd never forget them.

She grabbed clean clothes from her dresser and walked into the tiny bathroom attached to her bedroom. She'd take a shower and then she'd go raid the cupboards. There had to be a candy bar hiding somewhere.

It wouldn't take away the fear, but at least it would give her a little energy while she waited for Gavin to return.

One thing was for sure, she wasn't going to sleep. There might be an officer stationed downstairs, but she didn't trust anyone but herself to protect her kids.

SIX

Gavin took a long swig of coffee and tapped his pen against the conference table. It had been—he glanced at his watch—forty minutes since he'd decided to send Chase to Erin Eagleton's apartment. The girlfriend of the victim, Michael Jeffries, and a senator's daughter, she hadn't been there when Brooke had gone to question her. Hopefully, she was there now. They needed to hear her side of the story. Since none of the children at All Our Kids had been willing to admit to being near the Jeffries mansion, he was short witnesses and short a suspect. He needed both, and Erin might just be the key to that.

If she was a witness, they needed to speak with her, find out what she'd seen, what she'd heard.

If she was a suspect…

He fingered a photo of the pendant Chase had found and frowned. He couldn't imagine Erin pulling the trigger and killing her boyfriend, but that didn't mean she hadn't done it.

She'd been at the scene for sure.

They just had to put a time on that, and they couldn't until they questioned her and Harland.

He glanced at his watch again. As of twenty minutes

ago, Harland was out of surgery and in recovery. He was expected to survive, but he wasn't up to being questioned.

"Watching the time isn't going to make things happen more quickly," Isaac Black said as he thumbed through the crime scene photos Gavin had printed out. A former CIA operative, Isaac had been working with Capitol K-9 for a few years. He and his bomb detecting dog, Abby, had a good reputation for getting jobs done.

"It shouldn't have taken more than twenty minutes for Chase to get to Erin's place," Gavin responded.

"You know how traffic is in the city. One day it's easy driving. The next it's not." Isaac lifted a copy of the photo Gavin had been looking at and pointed at the pendant. "Seems to me, we should be putting an APB out on Erin Eagleton. If Chase is right about the locket being hers, there's no doubt she was at the crime scene. The sooner we get her into custody, the better."

"Being at the crime scene doesn't make a person guilty," Adam Donovan said.

"Doesn't make her innocent, either," Nicholas Cole responded quietly. Tall, with blond hair and pale brown eyes, he and his Doberman, Max, had proven themselves over and over again, their work ethic and teamwork making them an irreplaceable part of Capitol K-9.

"We'd better hope she has an alibi." Isaac set the photo of the pendant aside and lifted one of Erin. Taken from an online newspaper article, it showed her at some political event, her floor-length dress hugging her slender curves, her arm around Michael Jeffries. She smiled into the camera, the pendant she wore clearly the same as the one that had been found at the crime scene. "Her family isn't going to like that we're pulling her into this mess."

"We're not pulling her into anything," Gavin said,

pushing away from the conference table and striding across the room. He needed a long run and a hot shower to clear his head, but he wasn't going to get either.

Too bad. He needed to come up with a plan that was going to get them what they needed and get it quickly. Muddled thinking was not going to help with that.

Outside, the sun was just peeking over the trees, the sky deep purple and pink. He'd been working for nearly twenty-four hours, and he didn't think he'd be off the clock anytime soon. That was the nature of the job. One of the things he loved about it and one of the things Helena had hated. "Erin was at the scene," he continued. "She put herself into our investigation."

"We'll see how her senator father feels about that," Adam muttered. "I've got a feeling he's going to try to shut down our investigation into his precious little girl."

"If he does, Margaret will handle it. Our job—our *only* job—is to find the person who killed Michael Jeffries." Gavin turned back toward the conference table. Ten members of the fourteen-member K-9 team were there, all of them nursing coffee or soda, some of them with their dogs beside them, some without. He loved his team. Every member was as important as the next, and each one brought a special skill, a unique way of looking at things. When she'd put Capitol K-9 together, Margaret had chosen carefully and she'd chosen well.

"We'll be conducting this investigation like any other," he said. "Doesn't matter that the victim was the congressman's son. Doesn't matter that we might be stepping on some high-level toes. This is a murder investigation."

"It could be a double murder investigation," John Forester remarked. A newer member of the team, he'd been

brought in to replace his older brother, who'd been murdered a couple of years ago. The killer had never been found. It was a thorn in the side of Capitol K-9. One that Gavin hoped they'd one day remove. "Rosa Gomez didn't just fall off the cliff at President's Park. Anyone who thinks she did has his head buried so deep in the sand he can't see day from night."

Gavin thought the same, but the Gomez case wasn't theirs.

Yet.

If they could prove there was a connection, they'd have to take it over. Until then, they had to tread carefully. "I'm with you on that, John, but the DC police are handling the investigation. We need to keep our noses out of it until we have a definitive link."

John nodded, but he didn't look happy. "There's something big going on here, Gavin. I'm sure I'm not the only one who thinks so."

That was enough to get the team talking, their voices rising and falling as they discussed possibilities, suspects, reasons why Michael Jeffries, a guy who'd worked his entire adult life to protect the rights of others, would have been gunned down. Michael had been a good guy, a great guy, and everyone in the room knew it.

Gavin's cell phone rang, and he answered immediately.

"McCord here. What's up?"

"It's Chase. I'm at Erin's place. No sign of her. I spoke to a couple of neighbors. One remembers seeing her leave yesterday afternoon. She hasn't been back."

"The neighbors are sure of that?"

"As sure as they can be without going into the apartment. Want me to get a search warrant?"

"Yes."

"Good, because I already called Judge Simpson. He's getting it started. Should have it in a few hours. You want me to stick around here until then?"

"Yes. If she shows up, let me know, and call as soon as you have the search warrant in hand."

"You've got it." Chase disconnected, and Gavin shoved the phone back in his pocket. "Looks like our prime witness is on the run," he muttered.

"Or she's dead," Adam responded. "Have you thought about that possibility?"

"Trust me," Gavin muttered. "I've thought about all of them. You want to head over to her place, Adam? Wait with Chase and help him search the apartment once the warrant is in?"

"No problem."

"The rest of you can follow your regular schedule. I'll need Nicholas, John and Dylan to help me with protection shifts at All Our Kids. Margaret has already approved the overtime. Check your schedules," he said. "Make sure you're not on White House duty in the next few days. If you are, let me know, and we'll work around existing assignments. Everyone else, keep your eyes and ears open. I'll send out information regarding DNA evidence once it comes in. We have two different blood types collected at the scene. Glory took a nice chunk out of the perp's arm, so I'm assuming some of the blood is his. Hopefully that will point us in the right direction."

"Hopefully it will point us in *some* direction," Isaac muttered, standing and stretching. "Right now, we've got nothing but a body and a shooting victim."

"And a witness who may have seen the face of the killer. Cassie Danvers got a good look at the guy who

was on her back porch. I've already asked Margaret to call in a sketch artist. I'm heading back over to All Our Kids," Gavin added. "Hopefully a couple of hours of sleep has loosened their tongues."

"Bring doughnuts and juice," Nicholas suggested. "Kids love stuff like that. Plus, you get them all sugared up and it might get them so hyper they won't be able to control their tongues, the information could just spill out."

"Good idea. Since I'm planning on you running shift there tonight, I'll make sure they're all on sugar highs." Gavin snagged his pile of crime scene photos. "See you at seven."

"Hey!" Nicholas sputtered. "You didn't say anything about me working there tonight."

"I have now."

"I'm not good with kids!" he protested.

"Neither am I, and I'm spending all day with them."

Which meant they'd be awake and active and probably loud.

Gavin frowned. Maybe doughnuts weren't such a bad idea. If their mouths were full, they wouldn't be as likely to scream, shout, do any number of things that were bound to make him grind his teeth and want to beat his head against a wall.

It wasn't that Gavin didn't like kids. He did. He just hadn't spent much time interacting with them. His life was too busy, his work too demanding. It was the mantra Helena had spouted every day for the past six months of their dating relationship.

She'd been right.

He'd admit it. But his work mattered. The time he spent protecting the public at political events, protect-

ing politicians, protecting their families, was time well-spent. At least, in Gavin's opinion it was.

He could see why a girlfriend, wife, children might not put as much value on his job. Which was why he'd decided those things wouldn't be part of his life. He had no regrets about that. He didn't feel as if he'd be missing out. There were times, though, when he felt lonely, when he and Glory returned to his empty apartment, and he wondered what it would be like to return to a smiling face, a hug, a tender touch.

He shook the thought off as he dismissed the meeting and headed out into the parking lot. He'd stop home for a shower and a change of clothes, then head back to All Our Kids. There were probably half a dozen doughnut places in the vicinity. He didn't think Cassie would thank him for it, but he was going to stop and get a couple dozen of the sugary treats. It might not help, but it couldn't hurt. He needed to build a bond with the kids if he was going to get the truth out of them.

He thought about little Rachel with her curly blond hair and her big blue eyes. She'd looked pure as the driven snow, but she'd been lying through her teeth. He'd known it. Cassie had known it.

Someone else was lying, too. If he had to guess, he'd have said it was Tommy. Although he couldn't quite call it a lie since all the kid had done was shake his head. He'd also looked scared, his body trembling even as he'd refused to speak.

Had the little boy left All Our Kids? Had he walked the path to the congressman's backyard and seen something that had scared him into silence?

Gavin needed to get the truth out of him, because he

needed to find Michael's killer. Until he did, no one at All Our Kids would be safe.

"Cassie," someone whispered in her ear, warm breath ruffling the hair near her ear.

"I'm sleeping," Cassie muttered.

"If you were, you wouldn't be talking." Whoever it was didn't get the hint.

One of the kids for sure, but Cassie didn't open her eyes. "People talk in their sleep."

"Cassie!" The kid shook her shoulder. "The police officer is back."

"She never left," Cassie mumbled. K-9 police officer Brooke Clark had proven to be as conscientious, as kind and focused on her job as Gavin had been. No way would she have walked out on the job.

"Not her," the child—and Cassie wasn't planning to open her eyes, so she wasn't sure which one was whispering—said, "the hunky blue-eyed guy who was asking us all those questions."

Hunky?

Had to be Destiny, then.

Cassie forced her eyes open, and realized she'd fallen asleep at her desk, the side of her face pressed to cool wood.

"What time is it?" She groaned. She'd been up until sunrise, cleaning the kitchen and the foyer, scrubbing blood from the floor. Officer Clark had offered to call in a cleaning crew, but she hadn't been sure they could be there before morning. Cassie hadn't wanted the kids to wake to the mess. She'd wanted to do everything she could to make things look as normal as possible.

Not that there was anything normal about Cassie fall-

ing asleep at her desk. She'd been making a list of things that needed to be done. Back porch cleaned, kitchen window fixed. Stained tiles on the kitchen floor removed.

"Past time for Sunday school." Destiny's face was about two inches from Cassie's, her dark hair a wild mess of waves. She needed her bangs trimmed. Another thing for Cassie to put on her to-do list. "Guess that means we'll have to skip church today."

"Don't sound so happy about it." Cassie sat up, her neck muscles spasming. "We can always go to night service."

"And be out there where any guy with a gun could shoot one of us dead." Destiny's words were flippant, but there was no mistaking the fear in her eyes. She might act tough, but inside she was a scared little girl.

"No one is going to shoot any of us."

"That's not what Virginia said. She said we're all doomed."

"Virginia and I will have to have a little talk." Cassie smoothed her hand down the front of her cotton shirt. She should have worn a T-shirt and jeans, but she'd grabbed the first thing she'd seen when she'd opened her closet—a white cotton blouse with eyelet sleeves and a maxi skirt.

They definitely didn't hold up well to being slept in. There were so many wrinkles in the shirt, it looked as if it had been crumpled into a ball and shoved into the back of a drawer.

"Right now, she's talking to the hunk. They're downstairs in the living room, and Virginia said none of us could be in there with them. I think she has the hots for him."

"Destiny," Cassie warned. "First of all, no more re-

ferring to Captain McCord as hunky, hunk or hunkalicious."

"I didn't say hunkalicious."

"Not to anyone?"

"Well, maybe to Rachel," Destiny admitted.

"That's what I thought. Captain McCord is not—"

"He said we could call him Gavin," Destiny interrupted, her dark eyes sparkling with excitement. "And, he brought doughnuts. I think there must be fifty of them."

That explained why Destiny had come looking for Cassie.

"I take it you want my permission to eat a dozen of them?" Destiny was funny that way. She'd sneak food when no one was looking, but when other people were around, she followed all the rules. One doughnut. Two cookies. One handful of chips.

"Just one more. Or two. Or maybe three."

"Are you planning to wear that one on your face, too?" Cassie responded, wiping a smudge of chocolate off of Destiny's face. The young girl flinched, her cheeks red, her gaze dropping.

"I used a napkin, and Virginia said we could have the doughnuts."

"Was that before or after she said we were all doomed?" Cassie put an arm around Destiny's shoulder and led her out of the office.

"After," Destiny responded, her shoulders relaxing as they made their way downstairs. There were stories Destiny could tell about her life before she'd come to All Our Kids. Every once in a while, she opened up and let a little of the past slip out. Cassie let her go at her own pace, to reveal things when she was ready. The coun-

selor said she didn't talk about the past at all, but Cassie knew different. When Destiny trusted a person, she revealed pieces of her heart.

It was an honor to be one of the few people that she shared with, so Cassie never pushed her, never tried to get her to reveal more than she was comfortable with.

By the time they hit the second floor, Cassie could hear the other children. It sounded like field day during the heat of summer—eight voices all vying for the loudest-kid-in-the-house award. She already had a splitting headache and a stiff neck, but she forced a smile as she walked into the kitchen.

A pile of white boxes sat in the middle of the kitchen table, the kids—all in various states of undress—hovering around it. One of the boxes was open, the remnants of a chocolate doughnut in the bottom of it. The other doughnuts were either in hands or smeared across guilty faces. Seven little boxes of apple juice sat on the counter. One lay on the floor, the juice dripping out from the straw. Juan was sitting beside it, a mashed doughnut in one hand, a juice box in the other. He had chocolate smeared on his face, and the front of his shirt was soaked with juice.

He needed a bath. Stat.

And, Cassie needed to get the kids away from the sugar.

"Everyone, freeze," she commanded, and the entire bunch just kept doing what they were doing—shoving doughnuts into their mouths.

"Freeze means stop moving," she explained, as if that was going to do any good. "It also means if you don't freeze, you're going to spend the afternoon helping Mrs. Jordan clean out her garage."

Everyone stopped except for Juan. He was attempting to shove the entire fistful of doughnut into his mouth.

She scooped him up, wrested the chocolate doughnut from his hand. "I think you've had enough, buddy."

He patted her cheek, looked into her eyes.

"Where Mommy?" he asked, clear as a bell.

This was the part of the job she hated. It seemed she was always the bearer of bad news. The one who had to tell children that their parents or grandparents, their aunts or uncles couldn't make it for visitation because they were in jail or wasted or too busy to spend a half hour with family.

Of course, Juan's case was different.

His mother had loved him.

The fact that she'd died...or been killed...didn't change that. "Well, sweetie—"

"She's in Heaven. That's where she is—" David piped up, repeating what he'd heard Cassie say every time Juan asked where his mother was. He looked better than he had in a week, his skin less pallid, his eyes brighter. "And she probably has wings, too."

"Probably not, David. So how about you don't tell Juan that," Cassie chided.

"Maybe she does," he argued.

"Shut up!" Tommy snapped, his eyes flashing with irritation, his light brown hair puffing up around his head. He looked tired and crabby, not a hint of doughnut on his face or clothes.

"Don't be rude, Tommy," she said, and he scowled.

"He's the rude one! Telling a little kid lies like that."

"It's not a lie!" David insisted.

They were heading for a rip-roaring fight, and Cassie

was so tired she wanted to walk out of the room and leave them to it.

Too bad she couldn't.

"Boys, if you say one more word, I'm going to have to put you both in time-out."

They clamped their lips together and stared each other down.

Cassie sighed, then settled Juan into his high chair with a kiss on the cheek and his favorite little stuffed animal. She plugged in the coffeepot, hoping it brewed quickly. She needed caffeine. Fast!

"Cassie!" Virginia stepped into the kitchen, Gavin behind her. "I thought I heard you!"

Did you hear the kids? she almost asked, but she managed to swallow down the sarcasm.

"You did," she said instead.

Gavin's lips quirked, and Cassie was sure he'd heard the edge in her voice.

"Got a little out of hand in here, I see," he said, glancing around the kitchen, Glory edging in close to his leg.

The kids were all silent, their eyes focused on the shepherd. Not a peep out of any of them. Cassie wasn't even sure they were breathing.

"More than a little. In this house, doughnuts, juice and kids are usually a combination that need supervision."

"It was my fault, Cassie," Virginia said. "Gavin wanted to ask me a few questions, and I didn't want to wake you."

"It's okay. If you take the kids upstairs, I'll get the mess cleaned up. Then we can figure out what we're going to do with the rest of our day."

"Actually," Gavin said, "I was hoping I could speak

with Tommy and Rachel again. Tommy first, if that's okay."

She didn't have a choice, so she nodded. "Sure. Does that sound okay to you, Tommy?"

He took a deep breath, shrugged. "I guess."

"Do you want to talk in the office again?" Gavin asked. "Or the living room? Where will you feel more comfortable?"

"I don't care."

"Let's go in the living room." Cassie put her hand on Tommy's shoulder, but he shrugged away, running into the hall, his footsteps pounding on the wood floor.

She thought he was heading into the living room until she heard the front door open.

"Tommy! Stop!" she yelled, sprinting past Gavin and Glory, racing toward the door as it slammed shut. She yanked it open, and just caught sight of Tommy as he ran around the side of the house.

SEVEN

Cold March air slapped at her cheeks, the sunlight nearly blinding her as she jumped down the porch steps.

"Tommy! Come back here!" she shouted into the quiet morning, her pulse pounding loudly in her ears.

He didn't answer, and she ran the way she'd seen him go, her skirt tangling around her legs as she flew across around the house.

"Come back here right now, Thomas!" she yelled, but he'd disappeared. No sign of him in the yard. No hint of him at the edges of the property. He had to be there somewhere, though. He was fast for a seven-year-old, but not so fast that he should have been able to disappear so quickly.

She ran to the corner of the house, hoping she'd see him heading across the backyard. He wasn't there, and she felt a moment of such pure panic, she almost forgot what she was doing, who she was trying to find. Her mind was blank, her legs weak, everything inside her cold with fear.

He couldn't be gone. *Couldn't be.*

She whirled around, slammed into a hard chest. Warm hands settled on her waist as she looked up into Gavin's

face, into his blazing blue eyes. He looked frustrated, irritated, a little angry.

"Go back inside," he ordered, releasing his grip and stepping away. He had Glory on her lead, was surveying the area as if Cassie weren't still standing there, as if she'd already done what he'd told her to. As captain of the Capitol K-9 team, he was probably used to people obeying his orders.

It wasn't going to happen this time.

Tommy was Cassie's responsibility. She wasn't going back inside without him.

She didn't bother calling for the little boy again. He hadn't answered the first two times, and she doubted he was going to suddenly decide to answer now. He'd found a hiding place, and it had to be close. She just had to stop panicking and think like a seven-year-old. Shrubs butted up against the face of the house, trees dotted the yard, everything just beginning to bud, the nearly bare branches offering little in the way of cover. The tree line offered a little thicker foliage, the woods a quick and easy escape route for a scared kid. If he'd headed into the trees, there was no way she'd be able to find him easily.

Please don't let him have gone that way.

The prayer rang through her head as she scanned the tree line, tried to see into the shadowy depth of the forest. She'd never particularly cared for the woods. They were too dark, too quiet, too everything a girl from the city wasn't used to.

"Cassie," Gavin snapped, his voice so unexpected, she nearly jumped out of her skin.

"What?" She whirled to face him, realized that he was inches away, his dark hair glossy in the morning sunlight, his eyes blazing vivid blue. He'd shaved, and

she could see a faint scar on his jaw, another one near his temple.

"Go inside," he commanded, and there was no doubt that was exactly what it was—a command he expected to be obeyed.

"Not without Tommy."

His gaze sharpened, and she had the feeling there were a dozen things he was thinking, a dozen things he was trying hard not to say.

She braced herself, expecting that he'd lay into her, tell her that he was the one in charge. She'd heard it all before, remembered dozens of different police officers, in dozens of different situations, all of them eager to let her know that *they* were the ones who called the shots. Didn't matter if she was ten, eleven, twelve years old. Didn't matter if it was midnight and she was sound asleep in her bed at her grandmother's house. All that had ever mattered to the police was that they got what they wanted.

Gavin touched her shoulder, and it took everything inside of her not to flinch away. She wasn't a little kid anymore. She was an adult who'd learned the fine art of dealing with the authorities. She knew how to stand up for herself and for her kids.

"Someone tried to kill you last night, Cassie," he said. He could have been speaking to one of the kids, his voice was so gentle, his touch so light. "Have you forgotten that?"

"No," she mumbled, her throat tight, her eyes burning. If he'd continued to command and demand, she'd have been fine, but he'd changed tactics on her, looking at her the way he'd looked at each one of the kids when he'd interviewed them the previous night—with a soft-

ness in his gaze and in his face, a gentleness that she found surprising and sweet and just a little compelling.

She looked away, because her heart was beating way too fast. Not because of fear or anger. Because of Gavin. Because of the hard angles of his jaw and cheekbones and the softness of his expression, because of his vivid blue eyes and those two faint scars on his face.

"He's still at large," he said quietly. "And you're the only one who got a good look at him."

"You're not telling me anything I don't already know," she said, trying to sound confident and strong. Her voice was shaky, though, and she was annoyed by her weakness, by the strange urge she had to do what Gavin asked. She'd been making her own way in life for so long, she couldn't remember what it was like to depend on someone else. She didn't think she'd ever known what it was like. Only Miss Alice had ever been reliable, and she'd been nearly ninety when Cassie entered her home. She'd needed help as much as Cassie had needed love.

"He's going to have to take you down, Cassie. As long as you're alive, he's in danger." He touched the bruise on her cheek, his touch light and gentle.

"I know that, too." She stepped away, putting some distance between them. She'd known Gavin for three years. She'd watched him do a dozen jobs around the house, seen him in work clothes, seen him in dress clothes, seen him brush shoulders with high-powered politicians and with the parents of some of the children who'd been through All Our Kids' doors.

She'd known him, but she'd known nothing about him.

It probably would have been better if things had stayed that way, if she'd never looked straight into his bright

blue eyes, if she'd never seen the gentleness in his expression, the kindness in the way he dealt with her kids.

There was no way they'd be able to go back to the way they'd been—cordial acquaintances who didn't do much more than nod at each other. And, she wasn't happy about that.

She wasn't happy about anything that had happened in the past few hours. She walked around the side of the house and headed to the backyard. There was a swing set there, a slide, a small playhouse where the kids liked to hang out. If she were seven and scared, she'd go somewhere comfortable and comforting. The playhouse filled the bill.

"If you know all that—" Gavin broke into her thoughts, stepping up beside her, his dark jeans and dark jacket making him look rugged and tough and a little dangerous "—then you know why I want you to go inside."

"I know why, but that doesn't mean I can do it. Tommy is my responsibility."

"He won't be if you're dead."

"The guy who was here last night would be an idiot to come back today."

"And, you think returning while the police were at your house last night made him smart? Look what he did to get to you." He gestured to the back facade of the house, pointing at the boarded-up kitchen window, the back door that had been wrestled into place but still had a hole where a foot had kicked through the wood. "You think he won't come back during the day? You think he's not out in the woods waiting for an opportunity to strike again?"

"I *think* that you're not going to scare me into going inside."

"You've got eight kids depending on you, and someone wants you dead. If I've got to work at scaring you, Cassie, you've got a problem. Right about now, you should be terrified."

"I *am* terrified," she admitted. They'd reached the playhouse. Eight by ten and four feet tall, it butted up against the woods, the clapboard siding and pitched roof making it look like a tiny little home. Someone had crafted a door and put in windows. In the spring, Cassie always planted flowers in the miniature window boxes.

Glory sniffed the ground, nudged the door with her nose.

Gavin touched Cassie's arm.

"He's in there," he mouthed.

She nodded, relieved, anxious to get the little boy back inside. Anxious to be back inside herself. She was acting brave because she had to, but Gavin's words had lodged in her chest, sent icy chills up her spine.

Someone wanted her dead.

She'd known it before he'd said it, but somehow his words made it seem more real.

"Tommy," she called softly, pushing open the door and crouching so she could see inside. The kids brought all kinds of things into the fort—toys, stuffed animals, books. Cassie had dragged kids' chairs and a miniature table in there a couple of years ago, and during the spring and early fall, she let the kids with good grades take their books out to the playhouse to study.

"Go away," Tommy called, his voice muffled and thick. She could see him sitting against the far wall, knees pulled up to his chest, head down.

Had he been crying?

"Tommy, we need to go back inside. Captain McCord wants to talk to you."

"I don't want to talk to no one," Tommy sobbed.

"What's wrong, buddy?" She crawled into the fort, scooted around the table and chairs, sat beside him on the dirt floor.

"Go away," he muttered, not looking up as she slid an arm around his shoulders.

"You know I can't."

"You can do whatever you want. You're a adult."

"Okay, so I don't want to. Why are you crying?"

"I'm not crying!" he shouted.

"Lying about it doesn't make it not true. What's going on? You went out last night, didn't you?"

"No!" he said emphatically. She glanced across the small space, saw Gavin crouched in the doorway of the house, Glory nosing in beside him. He gestured for her to bring Tommy out, and she knew she had to. Whatever Tommy was thinking, whatever he was feeling, they could discuss it in the safety of the house.

"That's fine, then, but something is bothering you. Let's go inside. You can have another doughnut, and you can tell Captain McCord what you're so afraid of."

"No," he said with a little less energy.

"Why not? You love doughnuts."

"I don't like that old house. The window and door are broken. The bad man can get in again."

"Not while Glory is there," Gavin said.

"She can't always be there," Tommy said with a heavy sigh that made him sound old and jaded.

"My boss says she can. Margaret works directly with the president, so what she says goes."

"Really?" Tommy finally lifted his head, his face streaked with tears. He loved all things historical and everything that had to do with the government. At his age, that was unusual, but Cassie encouraged the interest, bringing him downtown as often as she could.

"Yes. Really."

"Did you meet the president?" he asked, and Gavin nodded.

"I've met him. I even spoke to him a couple of times."

"Wow! What's he like?"

"I'll tell you once we're inside. You're right about there being a bad man, Tommy. My job…and Cassie's… is to make sure you're safe. That'll be a lot easier to do inside the house."

Tommy hesitated, then started crawling to the door. Success! But not because of Cassie.

She wasn't sure how she felt about that, and she didn't have time to think about it.

She scooted out of the playhouse and took Tommy's hand. He was small for his age, thin and small-boned and a little fragile-looking. She had a soft spot for him. But, then, she had soft spots for all the kids who came through her door.

Most people assumed that she had taken the job because she wanted to help children. They assumed that she cared about the kids, that she wanted the best for them. They were right, but what they didn't seem to understand was that she loved them. That when they entered All Our Kids, they were her family. For however long they stayed there, she became their mother in every way that mattered.

"You nearly scared the life out of me, Tommy," she said as she led him across the backyard. Gavin and Glory

were right beside them, but she didn't feel safe. She felt exposed. "Please don't ever—"

Glory growled, her ears standing straight up as she turned her head toward the woods. Another growl, and she was tugging against the lead, snapping at something Cassie couldn't see, barking ferociously.

"Get down!" Gavin shouted, tackling Cassie and Tommy, bringing them both to the ground so quickly, Cassie wasn't even sure how they'd gotten there.

The first bullet slammed into the ground, bits of dirt flying into Gavin's face as he pulled his gun. The second whizzed just above Gavin's head. He aimed for the tree line, fired one round. Another.

Glory stayed beside him, her training preventing her from getting between him and the gunman. Cassie and Tommy were a different story. The little boy was sobbing hysterically, trying desperately to get up and run while Cassie tried just as desperately to keep him down, to cover him with her body.

If Gavin didn't take control quickly, she'd die trying to keep Tommy alive.

He fired a third round. No returning gunfire. The gunman had either been hit, taken cover or run.

Gavin was hoping for the first, but he wasn't banking on it. The guy was determined. That much was obvious. He wanted to take Cassie out, and he was going to do whatever it took to make that happen.

Gavin was going to make sure he wasn't successful. He called for backup, unhooked Glory's lead. The dog's ears were alert, her eyes trained on the woods, but she wasn't barking, wasn't giving any indication that they were in imminent danger.

"He's on the run," he muttered, turning so that he was face to face with Cassie. Her deep green eyes were wide, her face colorless. She had Tommy completely covered with her body, but the kid was continuing to fight her tooth and nail. "We need to get him in the house. Can you manage it?"

"Yes."

"Are you sure, Cassie?" He bit the words out, every minute that he was talking a minute that he wasn't chasing down the perp.

"Yes!" She rolled off Tommy, scooped him into her arms. The kid's mouth was open in a silent scream, his eyes huge. He'd snagged something as Cassie pulled him up. A rock or brick that he was clutching in his left hand. A puff of dusty earth trickled from his right.

"Go!" Gavin shouted, firing another round at the tree line as Cassie raced to the house, Tommy flailing and screaming in her arms. She was a small woman, and Gavin wasn't sure she could make it with a forty-pound kid, but somehow she managed to run up the porch steps, slam her shoulder against the broken door.

Once.

Twice.

The door gave, and she tumbled in.

He thought he heard her shouting something, but he was too busy issuing Glory's command to hear. She took off, nearly flying across the grassy yard as Gavin sprinted after her. His radio buzzed, the dispatcher asking for clarification of his location. He gave it quickly, the words panting out as he raced along the path that led to the congressman's property.

Was that where the perp was headed?

The place was still a crime scene, the area cordoned

off, but the police presence was gone, and the long drive-way that led to the house would be the perfect place for someone who wanted easy access to All Our Kids.

And an easy escape from it.

Was the perp's car parked there?

Glory was a hundred feet ahead, the sunlight stream-ing onto her dark coat as she raced through the woods. She knew where she was heading. She could hear what Gavin couldn't, sense what he couldn't. He'd come to count on her completely, to trust her implicitly. When she veered from the path, he followed, not calling her back, not doubting her direction.

She was moving through the trees, no hesitation, but no frantic barking, either. The danger was gone, and Glory knew it. She'd keep going until she was called off, but she'd lost her frenetic edge.

They were close to the road that meandered through Harland's ritzy neighborhood. Gavin could see the pave-ment through the trees, see a glint of sunlight reflecting on metal. No one parked on the street. Not in a neigh-borhood like this one. But there was a car on the road. Gavin could see it clearly as he tore through thick foli-age, sprinted up a shallow rise.

The perp's car?

He hoped so. He wanted the guy in custody today. Not tomorrow. Not next week.

The car engine revved as he stepped out onto the pavement. Glory growled, her body going tense again, her ears pricked, her dark eyes focused on the black Toy-ota parked in a small grassy area to the left of the road. It jumped forward, speeding toward them so quickly, Gavin didn't have time to fire a shot.

He dove for cover, sliding down the embankment on

his back, the sound of a car slamming into one of the trees filling his ears as he turned onto his stomach, and fired a shot that hit the fender of the car.

Tires squealed, and he knew the guy was backing up, getting ready to speed away.

Gavin scrambled up to the road, gun still drawn, and nerves alive with adrenaline. He wanted to catch a glimpse of the gunman, needed to let the guy know that he had him in his sights.

Glory panted a few feet away, ready to lunge. Ready to do everything in her power to protect and serve.

He called her back as they stepped onto the road again.

The car was already heading away, speeding along the road, heading toward the entrance to the community. Gavin fired another shot, smiling grimly as a back tire blew out.

The perp kept going, the car nearly airborne as it raced over a bump in the road and disappeared around a steep curve.

They'd lost him.

Gavin holstered his firearm, frustration eating at his gut.

They'd been close, and that made losing the guy even worse.

He called in the color and make of the car, following the path it had taken around the curve in the road. The car wouldn't get far with a blown tire. That gave him a small sense of satisfaction, but it wasn't enough. They weren't far from the heart of DC. The guy would probably abandon his vehicle and walk out of the neighborhood.

A Capitol K-9 patrol car sped into view, slowing as it approached, the driver's side window sliding down.

Brooke Clark peered out at him. "Need a lift?" she asked. A former army captain, she had a small frame that belied her strength and abilities. More than one criminal had been fooled into thinking she couldn't do her job and do it well. Each and every one of them had regretted the assumption.

"You're supposed to be off duty," he responded. But, he opened the back hatch of the vehicle, let Glory jump in with Brooke's golden retriever, Mercy, before he walked around to the passenger side of the vehicle and climbed in.

"I was. I filed some paperwork at headquarters and was on my way home when the call came in. I was halfway here, so I came." She shrugged. "DC police are looking for the black Toyota. I figured I'd be more help at All Our Kids then driving around looking for a car. Mercy is great at evidence detection, but neither of us are experts at tracking."

"You hear anything from Chase while you were at headquarters?" he asked as she turned the vehicle around, heading to the long driveway that led to All Our kids.

"Last I heard, he was still waiting for the search warrant."

"That's a long wait." Way longer than usual. If it didn't come through soon, Gavin was going to have to make some calls. Or have his boss do it.

"We're talking about a senator's daughter," Brooke pointed out.

"And?"

"No one wants the media circus a search of her apartment is going to bring. Either that, or Erin's daddy got wind of what was going on and called in some favors."

"Doesn't matter how many favors the senator has to call in. We'll get the search warrant. We have probable cause. No attorney can argue against our evidence for long." Gavin had no patience for politics, and he didn't believe in granting favors to people based on the social circles they moved in.

"I hope you're right," she responded, as she turned into the driveway of All Our Kids. "We need access to that apartment."

"You think we're going to find something incriminating?" he asked.

"A woman who routinely returns to her apartment doesn't just decide not to go home one night. Not unless she has a really good reason to stay away." She parked the car, turning to face Gavin, the ends of her dark hair brushing the collar of her shirt. "I'm interested to know what Erin's disappearance means. Did she run off because she saw something? Did she run because she's guilty? Did someone take her?"

"We don't know that she's disappeared. She might have gone out of town or spent the night at a friend's house."

"Come on, Gavin," she scoffed. "Her boyfriend is dead. That's all over the news. Unless she's in a cabin out in the middle of nowhere without access to the internet, she's heard about it. So why hasn't she called the police, checked in with the congressman, done anything that a girlfriend would do if she found out the man she loved was dead?"

"Those are good questions." He didn't have any answers. Yet. But he planned to get them.

"They're *worrisome* questions. We've got a lot more that we don't know than that we do. I don't like it."

"The whole situation is *worrisome*, Brooke. And, I don't like it, either," he responded, opening the door and getting Glory out of the back. "We've got eight kids and two adults in this house, and a blatantly aggressive perp. He'll keep coming back. Doesn't matter how many dogs, how much police presence we have on the ground. He'll find a way to get to Cassie and the kids."

"I was thinking the same." Brooke put Mercy on the lead, and met Gavin's eyes. "I guess you've got a plan to keep them safe?"

"We've got a couple of safe houses. I'm going to put in a call to Margaret. Get cleared to use one of them."

"It better be a big house," Brooke responded. "Because I don't think there's any way you're going to separate that group. Not if Cassie has anything to say about it."

She was right about that, and Gavin knew it.

It was going to be difficult enough to convince Cassie to pack the kids up and move them. There was no way she'd agree to have the kids separated into groups.

The three-story brick house seemed to glow in the bright sunlight, the windows gleaming, the porch whitewashed and spotless. It should have been a haven to the children living within its walls, but the sanctuary had been breached, and the kids were terrified. Gavin had sensed their fear, had felt it as he'd offered the kids doughnuts and juice, tried to make small talk with them and make a connection that would help them feel comfortable enough to open up to him.

He walked up the porch stairs, surprised when the door flew open and Virginia ran out, her eyes wide, her face pale.

"You're here! Hurry up! She's bleeding to death!" she shouted before turning on her heels and dashing back inside.

EIGHT

"I am not bleeding to death," Cassie mumbled for the fifteenth time, the words muffled by the wad of paper towel she was holding to her head. Tommy was small, but his fists were mighty. Especially when he had a rock in one of them. The blood splattered all over her shirt was proof of that.

She didn't dare look in the powder room mirror. Virginia had taken one look at her face and started screaming hysterically. The kids had scattered to the winds, running upstairs and into their rooms, Rachel carrying poor Juan who was screaming almost as loudly as Tommy. Only Virginia and Destiny had remained, one of them looking shell-shocked and scared, the other hollering for help that wasn't going to come.

If Cassie hadn't had blood running down her temple she'd have told Virginia to calm down for the sake of the kids. As it was, she'd had to find a way to staunch the bleeding without any help from her assistant.

"Are you sure?" Destiny hovered in the doorway, the phone in one hand, a baseball bat in the other. For such a young girl, she had a good head on her shoulders. She didn't usually panic and was helpful when help was most needed. "Virginia said—"

"How about we stop talking about what Virginia said for a while?" she muttered, the coppery taste of blood in her mouth. She'd already had a headache. Being slapped in the temple with a fist-sized rock hadn't made it any better.

"But—"

"Cassie!" Virginia yelled. "Are you okay? I found some help."

"I don't need help," she called. "I'm fine."

"You're not fine! You bled all over the kitchen." Virginia peeked into the powder room, her eyes wide and filled with fear. "You're still bleeding, aren't you? How much blood can a person lose before she passes out?" she asked no one in particular.

Cassie sighed, and kept pressing on the two-inch gash in her temple. She wasn't going to bleed to death, but she hoped to avoid stitches. The kids were traumatized enough. If she had to make a trip to the ER, they'd be even more upset.

"A lot," a man said.

Not just any man, either. Gavin. Cassie recognized the voice, bracing herself as he stepped into view.

He'd put his life on the line for her and for Tommy, positioning his body so that it was between them and the gunman. Maybe the wound to her head was worse than she thought, because looking at him standing in the doorway of the powder room, his eyes bright blue and somber, she felt something melt in the region of her heart.

She turned away, catching her reflection in the mirror.

She looked like she felt—ragged. Blood stained her cheek. Her hair stood up in a hundred different directions. She had dark circles under her eyes and dirt on her chin.

It didn't matter. She had no one to impress. Nowhere to go. Her life was her job, her kids. That's the way she wanted it.

For some reason, though, she had the absurd urge to wash her face, tame her hair.

She frowned. Her reflection frowned back.

"Cassie?" Gavin stepped into the small room, and it suddenly felt tiny, his large frame taking up more than its fair share of space. "What happened? Were you hit by shrapnel?"

"Nothing that glamorous." She forced herself to smile. "I got beaned in the head by a rock-wielding, panic-stricken seven-year-old."

"Mind if I take a look?" He moved her hand before she could say one way or another, and probed at the gash. "A couple of stitches wouldn't hurt."

"They wouldn't help, either. I've got some butterfly bandages in the medicine cabinet. I'll just slap a couple on, and we'll be good to go."

"You need to stop the bleeding first, wash it out." He tucked a couple of strands of hair behind her ears, reaching past to run the water in the sink. She could feel the heat of his body through her blouse, feel the firmness of his bicep as it brushed her arm. She wanted to step back, but there was nowhere to go, and she just stood there like a ninny while he wet the cloth, dabbed at her face, gently wiping the blood from her cheek, the dirt from her chin.

She could have closed her eyes, and just let him do what he was doing, because she suddenly had no energy, her legs weak with the aftermath of fear and adrenaline.

"Don't pass out on me now, Cas," he said quietly, and

she shook her head, trying to force some blood back into her brain.

"I never pass out."

"Good to know." He smiled, and her heart gave a funny little jerk.

"Is she going to be okay?" Virginia asked, her voice wobbling.

"I don't see why she wouldn't be. Can you go find those butterfly bandages?" Gavin dabbed the area around the gash with the cold cloth.

"Of course!" Virginia raced away, her feet pounding on the stairs.

"Good idea, giving her a job to do," Cassie conceded. "She does better when she's got something to focus on."

"I've noticed. Hold this." He grabbed her hand, pressing it to the cloth. "How about we go in the living room, so you can sit down while we wait for Virginia?"

"I'll bleed all over the couch."

"The dining room, then. I think the kitchen door is still down, and I don't want you anywhere near the back of the house until we get the perimeter of the yard secured."

She didn't want to bleed all over the dining room floor, either, but she had to admit, she was feeling a little light-headed. "Did you find the guy who was shooting at us?"

"No," he said grimly, his hand cupping her elbow as they walked out of the bathroom.

She wasn't going to admit it. Especially not with Destiny standing a few feet away, the baseball bat still clutched in her hand, her expression tight and unreadable, but she needed the support.

"Can you check on Juan, Destiny?" she asked as she passed the young girl. "And Tommy?"

"Tommy is a punk. He should be grounded for a month, and I'm not checking on him, because I don't care if he's buried under the entire pile of his stupid stuffed animals," Destiny responded, her chin wobbling, her eyes filling with tears Cassie knew she wouldn't shed.

"He didn't hit me on purpose. You know that."

"Doesn't matter. He should have been more careful. I'll check on Juan, but I'm not saying one word to Tommy ever again." She stomped up the stairs, her footsteps ringing through the too-quiet house.

The kids were probably hiding under beds and huddling in closets.

Or maybe not.

Most of them had come from homes where violence was the norm rather than the exception.

"It's going to be okay," Gavin said as he pulled out a dining room chair, pressing her down into it.

She sat, because she was exhausted, because her head hurt and her stomach ached, and she thought she might just do what she'd said she wouldn't—pass out.

Outside, sirens screamed, people shouted, an entire world of chaos was happening. She could hear it, but she tuned it out. There was nothing she could do to help. She'd given the best description she could of the man who'd been on the back porch, she'd cooperated in every way she could, but the guy was still free. That was something the police had to deal with.

What she had to deal with were eight traumatized kids, a hysterical assistant and a head that just would not seem to stop bleeding. She pressed the cloth tighter against the wound, wincing as it dug into the gash.

"You and the kids can't stay here. You know that, right?" Gavin sat in the chair next to hers, turned so that they were face to face. He looked relaxed, his elbows resting on his knees as he leaned forward to look into her eyes. She knew he wasn't. There was tension around his mouth, a hard edge to his gaze. He had an agenda. She wasn't sure she wanted to be part of it. She also wasn't sure she had a choice.

"I hadn't thought much further than getting through the next few minutes, getting the kids calmed down and going back to our routine," she hedged, because leaving All Our Kids had never occurred to her.

"It might be time to think a little farther. Even with guard dogs and twenty-four-hour protection. Even with the best security the city has to offer, you and the kids are in danger here."

"As long as we stay inside—" She started to argue, but he raised a hand, cutting off her words.

"We tried that, remember? And one of your kids ran outside and nearly got all three of us killed."

"Tommy didn't nearly get us killed. The guy with the gun did."

"You're putting up straw men, Cassie," he said calmly. "And it's not going to change the situation you're in. One of the kids was out last night. I think we can both agree to that. The guy who killed Michael saw him over at the congressman's house."

"We don't know that for sure."

"Look." He leaned in close, his eyes blazing. "You can bury your head in the sand or you can face the facts. One of the kids saw something. *You* saw something. You two are key witnesses in a murder case, and the perpetrator is still on the loose. None of you are going to be

safe here. The guy knows how to use a gun. He had an accelerant with him last night. For all we know, he's gone off somewhere to build a bomb that he can toss into your living room window or onto your front porch."

She hadn't thought about that.

Hadn't considered all the ways the guy could get to them. Not just through a door or a window. He could throw a bomb, detonate an explosive, set the house on fire.

She shuddered.

She hated to do it, because the kids needed the security of their routine. But she couldn't risk their lives.

"All right," she finally said. "If you've got a safe place for us, I'll pack the kids up and we'll head out."

He smiled, a real smile, a warm smile. The kind of smile that could make a woman look twice. "Good."

"You may not be saying that after you get my eight kids into the safe house." She pulled the cloth from her head. Blood didn't pour down her temple, so she thought the bleeding had stopped.

"I like that," he said, and she touched her temple.

"What's to like about a gaping wound on a woman's head?"

He chuckled, a deep quiet rumble that went straight to her heart. "Not that, Cassie. The fact that you think of these kids as yours. Not every foster parent feels that way."

"Not every foster parent has been a foster kid," she responded, doing everything in her power not to look right in his eyes. She didn't have time for flirtations, didn't have time for relationships. Her job had been the death of her last relationship, and she wasn't willing to go through the effort of connecting with someone, find-

ing common ground, falling in love only to have it not work out.

There was too much pain in that, and she figured she'd been through enough pain in her life. God had brought her out of it, and He'd brought her to All Our Kids. She was content with that.

"You're right. I don't think any of mine were," Gavin responded, and she made the mistake of glancing his way, looking into his vivid blue eyes. And, then, of course, she couldn't look away.

"How long were you in the foster system?" she asked, curious despite all the warning bells that were going off in her head. Bells that were ringing loudly and telling her that she'd better keep her distance or she might find herself in deeper than she wanted to be.

"The better question might be *how long wasn't I in it*?" he responded. "I was in ten different placements before I turned twelve. By the time I was fifteen, I'd pretty much run out of options."

"So, you ended up here?"

"I ended up picking the pocket of Harland Jeffries while I was on a field trip to the National Monument."

"No way!" Virginia gasped as she walked into the room, a first-aid kit in her hands. "I'd never believe something like that about you, Gavin."

Cassie could. She could picture him as a teenager, sullen, angry at everyone and everything, not caring about anything but getting back at the world. He wasn't that boy now, but she could see it in the sharpness of his gaze, hear it in the things he hadn't said.

"Believe it," he responded. "That's how I met Harland, and it's how I ended up in All Our Kids."

"How is Harland?" Cassie asked.

"Recovering well, the last I heard. I'll check in on him later this afternoon. I'd have done it sooner, but I've been a little preoccupied." He took a couple of butterfly bandages from the kit and pressed them to her forehead.

It hurt, but she didn't complain. She had other things to do. Like help the kids pack their bags.

She brushed Gavin's hands away and stood on legs that were a little shaky for her liking. "If I'm going to move eight kids to a new house, I've got to get packing."

"They won't need a lot. A couple of sets of clothes. Maybe a favorite toy. I'll make the call and put in a request for some kid-friendly foods, soaps, diapers."

"Do you really think these kids are going to leave any of their belongings behind?"

He ran a hand along the back of his neck. "Right. Let them pack what they want. We'll take as many cars as we need."

"I've got a fifteen-passenger van, Gavin. Plenty of room for everyone and everything." She walked toward the stairs, pleased that her legs didn't collapse out from under her.

"It would be, but you're not going to be taking your van."

"Of course I am. How else are we going to get the kids out of here?"

"Separate cars. A couple of kids in each of them. The less notice we get, the happier I'll be," he responded.

"But—"

"Would you rather the guy who just tried to kill you and Tommy see us all leaving? Would you rather he try to follow us or maybe take a potshot at the van?"

"You're assuming he's still around."

"I don't assume," he responded sharply, his eyes hard

as stone. "I imagine every possible scenario and I plan accordingly."

She didn't want to concede, because she didn't want the kids traveling in different cars. Just like she'd told him, they were her kids, her responsibility, the only family she had.

Then again, she didn't want them hurt. Or worse.

"All right," she said. "We'll go to the safe house. We'll take separate cars. But, I'll tell you one thing we're not going to do. We're not leaving Tommy's stuffed animal collection behind. He needs it to sleep, and since I don't want to spend an unspecified amount of time being sleepless with him, I need it too."

Gavin blinked. Twice. "Sure. Why not?"

Maybe because the collection was a hundred stuffed animals and growing. And maybe because the stuffed animals didn't come from the store, they came from Dumpsters and piles of trash and often smelled like skunk mixed with cadaver until they'd been washed ten times.

Cassie didn't bother explaining.

She had a lot to do. Not just packing and getting kids moving, explaining why they had to leave, where they were going to go, that they'd all be together.

That was important to her kids. They might not be a conventional family, but they were all each other had.

NINE

Obviously, Gavin should have said no when Cassie insisted that Tommy be allowed to bring all his stuffed animals to the safe house.

Obviously, she knew it.

She stood behind five overflowing boxes and smiled. "That's it. All one hundred of them."

"You're sure about that?" he asked dryly, eying the boxes, the woman, the little boy who was standing at her side. The other kids were in the foyer, carrying backpacks and a pillowcase stuffed with belongings. Some had books or toys. Little Juan Gomez had a bottle in one hand and a fistful of Virginia's hair in the other.

Tommy had more.

Lots more.

He had a backpack, a duffle, a pillowcase and the boxes.

No wonder it had taken Cassie two hours to get everyone packed. She'd probably spent the majority of her time getting Tommy's things together.

"I don't know," the young boy said. "Maybe there is one more. Maybe I left one under the bed. I think I did, Cassie. I think I did!" He darted back up the stairs, and Cassie sighed.

"Smooth move, Gavin. I'd finally convinced him that we had everything, and now we're back at the drawing board," she said, hefting the closest two boxes. "We may as well get these into one of the cars while we're waiting. He may be a while."

"He's checking under the bed. How long can that take?" He took the boxes, not because he thought she was too weak to carry them herself, but because Mrs. Simons would have had his head if she'd known he'd done anything else. Housemother at All Our Kids during the years Gavin was there, she'd had a kind heart and a will of steel. Aside from Harland, she'd influenced his life more than anyone.

"Not long, but then he'll have to check in the closet and in the dresser and in the tub. He'll probably check the entire second level before he comes down. He's a little OCD that way." She lifted two of the remaining boxes, her ponytail sliding over her shoulder. She'd changed clothes, replacing the blood-stained shirt and skirt with a soft-looking T-shirt and well-worn jeans. She'd also washed the blood off her face and out of her hair. The bandages pulled at the skin of her forehead, highlighting the goose egg and bruise she was sporting.

"Maybe I should go up and help him look?" Virginia suggested. "I don't know about everyone else, but being in this house is making my skin crawl. I mean, think about it—"

"We'd all rather not." Cassie cut her off. The statement was matter-of-fact rather than frustrated, and Virginia didn't seem at all fazed by it. She bounced Juan on her hip, murmuring something to him under her breath. The poor kid had been through a lot, and Virginia seemed bent on mothering him through it. She was good with

all the children. That had to be the reason Cassie kept her around. It certainly wasn't for her ability to respond well during crises.

"I'm just saying, Cassie. The sooner we leave, the happier I'll be."

"Then, let's start packing things into the cars." Cassie reached for the doorknob as if she thought she could just walk outside, go about her life the way she had before one of her kids had snuck out and been seen by a murderer.

"Hold on." Gavin nudged her hand away. Beside him, Glory shifted. She knew they were getting ready to head out, and she was anxious to go. "I'll pack everything in the cars."

"How many cars?" Cassie asked, edging close to him as he opened the door. He could feel the heat of her body, the brush of her arm against his; he could smell a sweet flowery scent that reminded him of honeysuckle and spring rain.

"Three. All driven by K-9 team members. You, Tommy, Rachel and Destiny are coming with me." He had a reason for that, and he was sure Cassie knew it. She eyed him for a moment, then shrugged.

"That's fine with me. If we ever get Tommy into the car."

"I am not riding with Tommy!" Destiny protested. She had fewer belongings than the other kids. Just a backpack. No pillowcase stuffed with things. No extra books, dolls or toys. She looked to be twelve or thirteen, but her eyes were old, the wariness in them something Gavin had seen dozens of times on the streets of DC.

"Sorry, Destiny," he said. "You don't have a choice."

"I have choices," she spat, glaring at him. "I can just…

go somewhere else. I can run away. Then, I can do what I want."

"True," Cassie said easily. "But, I'd miss you terribly if you did. Now, how about we all just get ourselves together and get this done? I, for one, could use a hot cup of coffee and some homemade cookies. You want to help me make some, Destiny?"

"Is there going to be a kitchen in our new place?"

"A big one." Gavin had made it very clear to Margaret that they needed more than the usual safe house. Not an apartment. Not a condo. Not a brownstone in the heart of DC. They needed space. Inside and out. She'd come through. Just like she always did.

"Then I guess I can ride with Tommy," Destiny sighed.

"Great." Gavin opened the door and stepped out into cool March air. There were DC police everywhere, K-9 teams combing the woods for evidence. He could see Brooke and Mercy crisscrossing a small area at the edge of the front yard. If they found something, he'd know it before anyone else.

Right now, his focus was on getting Cassie and the children to a safe location. Once he'd done that, he could return to the house and help process the scene.

He jogged down the porch stairs and opened the door of his SUV. He'd thought he'd have plenty of space for two adults, three kids and a dog, but the boxes were going to be challenging. He slid them onto the backseat floor, then grabbed the other two from Cassie's hands.

"What's the deal with these, anyway?" he asked as he shoved both into the hatchback next to Glory's kennel.

"What's the deal with any of the stuff any of the kids

have." She shrugged. "They don't have control of much in their lives, so they control their things."

"He's got a lot of things." He signaled for Glory to enter her kennel, and she jumped in, settling down for the ride.

"And a lot of baggage. You should understand that, Gavin."

He did.

He just wasn't all that happy about dealing with it. Not when there was so much at stake. One man dead. Another injured. A woman missing.

And then there was Rosa Gomez.

Dead, too.

Under suspicious circumstances.

That's what the DC police were saying.

A car pulled into the driveway and slowly moved toward the house. Gavin stepped in front of Cassie. Not because he thought the perpetrator would be foolish enough to drive up and gun her down, but because he didn't believe in taking chances any more than he believed in coincidence.

"Who is it?" she whispered, leaning around him, her braid falling against his arm as she tried to get a look.

"I don't know." Another police officer maybe. Or one of Gavin's team members.

The car pulled up behind his SUV—black sedan with government tags. He knew the car, was surprised to see it.

"Harland," he murmured, taking Cassie's hand and tugging her to the vehicle as the back passenger door opened and Harland Jeffries got out. Arm in a sling, face haggard from grief and pain, he looked a decade older than he was, his gray hair nearly white in the sunlight.

"Gavin," he said, his voice breaking. "Michael's gone."

"I know. I can promise you I'm going to do everything in my power to bring his murderer to justice."

Harland nodded, somehow weaker and frailer than Gavin had ever expected him to be. "I know you will. Margaret assured me the team is on the case."

"How about we go inside, Harland?" Cassie wove her arm through the congressman's. "You need to sit down."

"I need to find my son's killer," he muttered, but he let himself be led up the porch steps.

"Heel!" Gavin commanded Glory. She jumped out of the kennel, taking her place beside him as he followed Cassie and Harland into the house.

The kids were still waiting in the foyer, and their eyes widened as the congressman walked in. Gavin had no doubt they knew Harland. He made it a habit of visiting All Our Kids, of being part of the lives of the kids who stayed there.

"Okay!" Virginia called from the top of the stairs. "We've got everything, and we're sure about it!"

She was halfway down the steps when she realized Harland was there. She stopped short, her cheeks going a bright shade of pink.

"Congressman Jeffries!" she breathed. "What an honor!"

Tommy didn't seem to think it was an honor. He stayed behind Virginia, his dark hair barely visible.

"It's an honor for me, Virginia. You know how much I care about these kids." Harland smiled, moving into the living room and taking a seat on the sofa. "I heard you were going to be away for a while, so I thought I'd better come visit."

Margaret must have told him about the move to a safe house. In typical Harland fashion, he was going to make sure the kids were okay before they left.

"That was really kind of you, Harland," Cassie said. "But you should have stayed in the hospital. You're still recovering."

"The doctor released me this morning. After Margaret's call, I thought I'd better stop here before I went home." He met Gavin's eyes. "It looks like you have everything under control, but I thought it might help if I talked to the kids myself."

"Sure." Gavin was willing to try anything to get the kids to talk.

"Would you like some coffee?" Virginia offered, little Juan still in her arms. He looked at Harland. Reached for him.

"Mama!" he yelled, and Harland visibly flinched.

"Two deaths in two days." He shook his head. "It's too much. The poor child. With no mother."

And me with no son.

He didn't say that. Harland wasn't that kind of guy. But, Gavin thought he heard it, thought he saw it in the depth of Harland's eyes.

"I'm so sorry for your loss," Cassie said, sitting down next to the aging congressman, putting her arm around his shoulder like he was one of her kids.

"Thank you, my dear. It's difficult." Harland squeezed the bridge of his nose, and Gavin knew he was holding back tears. "I just wish that I'd seen…" He looked at the kids who were watching wide-eyed and maybe a little afraid. "Anyway, that isn't what I came to talk to you about. The thing is, I heard from the police that one of you children might have been on my property last night."

"Of course that's why you're here," Destiny snapped. "Adults never come around just because they care. They always come because—"

"Now is not the time, Destiny," Cassie said, an edge of weariness to her voice.

"It's okay," Harland said, patting Cassie's arm. "This is tough on the kids, I know that. But, I wanted to reiterate what Captain McCord and his team have been saying. If one of you was on my property last night, you're not in trouble. There will be no punishment. No ramifications." He looked at each child one by one.

Gavin did the same, focusing on the two that he most suspected. Rachel had her thumb in her mouth, a childish and young gesture for a child her age. He thought it was a probably a hold-over habit, something she only did when she was under incredible stress.

Tommy stood beside Virginia, his eyes trained on the ground, his expression blank. He didn't look at Harland. He didn't look at any of the adults in the room.

Harland sighed into the silence, squeezing the bridge of his nose again. "We all make mistakes, and kids tend to make a few more than adults. If any of you were at my place last night, if any of you saw what happened to my son…" He stopped, cleared his throat. "It's okay to say so."

Not a peep out of anyone.

Not that Gavin had expected there to be, but he felt a moment of disappointment, a moment of impatience. One of them had seen something. He knew it, but he couldn't force the truth out of their mouths.

Maybe being away from All Our Kids would loosen their tongues. The doughnuts and juice certainly hadn't.

Someone rapped on the front door, and an officer

opened it. Brooke stepped in, Mercy on the lead beside her. "Congressman Harland," she said, walking into the living room. "I thought that was your car."

"I had my assistant bring me. She's waiting in the car." He stood, wincing a little at the movement. "And, she's probably getting impatient. My discharge instructions didn't include stopping for visits."

"I'm glad you stopped by," Brooke said. "We wanted to clarify the description you gave to the first responding officer last night."

They'd already verified it, but Gavin knew what Brooke was doing. It was possible details of the night had been lost to Harland's trauma and grief and that a little distance, a little time, might allow him to remember more.

"I'll walk you two out," Gavin said.

"Me, too," Cassie added.

"Sorry." He put a hand on her arm before she could leave the living room. "We have some details of the case to discuss with the congressman. It's best if you wait here."

"You're kidding, right?" She raised a dark red brow, her emerald eyes clear and bright despite a nearly sleepless night. She was pale, though, her bruises standing out against her makeup-less skin.

"Why would I be?"

"You rushed us, and now you want us to wait? With a toddler? And a five-year-old? And a bunch of overtired, overstimulated kids?"

"I'm sorry," Gavin responded. He hadn't thought of that angle. But, then, he'd spent the past few years concentrating on his job. He'd devoted everything he had to Capitol K-9, because he owed it to Harland to make

good on the opportunities he'd been given and because he'd been sure that was what God wanted him to do.

But, maybe, being so devoted to work had made him a little less understanding of other people's lives.

He eyed the children, all of them watching him with various levels of distrust.

"I'll be quick. I promise."

"If you're not," Cassie called as he walked outside. "I'm sure the kids will make me pay for it, and then *I* will have to make *you* pay."

Her threat made him smile.

She was a funny lady. Smart, kind and firm enough to set the boundaries and hold tough to them. That was important in the job she did. Gavin knew it. His days with Mrs. Simons and her motley crew of foster kids had taught him just how important kindness and boundaries were.

Harland was already in his car by the time Gavin walked outside, Brooke standing near the open sedan door.

She turned as he approached, her muscles tense, her expression hard. "We may have a bigger problem than we think, Gavin. Remember Cassie's description of the perpetrator?"

"Average height. Blond hair. Blue eyes. Looked apathetic. Like he could take someone's life and not feel guilty about it?"

"The person I saw wasn't tall," Harland said. "He was maybe five-foot-eight."

"You're sure, Harland?" he asked, not because he didn't believe the congressman, but because he'd rather not believe they had two different perpetrators. That complicated things, opened the investigation up to more

than just a disgruntled employee or unhappy constituent, made it likely that this wasn't about one person's vendetta but, rather, a team effort.

But, effort to what?

As far as Gavin knew, Harland didn't step on political toes. He was firm and a little stern, but he was well-liked by his constituents and respected across partisan lines. Michael might have made enemies in his job as an attorney, and if he were the only victim, Gavin might have thought that the attack was aimed at him, that Harland had just been in the wrong place at the wrong time.

But Rosa was dead, too, and DC police were leaning toward murder.

"Of course, I'm sure," Harland snapped, then sighed and ran a hand over his hair. "Sorry. I'm a little—"

"You don't have to apologize, and I'm not questioning your testimony. I'm just verifying it. We have two different descriptions. Either one of you is mistaken in what you saw, or we're dealing with two different perps."

Harland frowned. "I know what I saw. I didn't see a face or hair color. I'm not even sure about body type. But, I've got a couple of new cherry trees in the backyard. They were all around seventy inches tall when the gardener planted them. The person who shot my son was at least a few inches shorter than that."

Not good.

"We could be talking about two people, then. I'm going to have Cassie meet with a sketch artist. We can plug the sketch into the FBI's face recognition system. Once—if—we get an ID, we can bring him in. Maybe he'll have more to tell us about what happened."

"I hope you're right." Harland frowned. "You'll need a really good sketch artist. I might be able to pull some

strings, get the FBI's top man to do the job. It could take a couple of days, but the wait might be worth it for the quality of the image."

Gavin wasn't sure he wanted to wait, but he wasn't willing to turn down the offer, either. "Tell you what, Harland. You see what you can arrange. I'm going to talk to Margaret and the team, decide if we're willing to risk a couple of extra days."

"We *will* have the kids and Cassie in a safe house," Brooke pointed out. "That will buy us some time."

Maybe. But Gavin wasn't counting on it.

He said goodbye to Harland and hurried back into the house. He'd need to speak with Cassie. Find out exactly how certain she was of the description she'd given.

Cassie needed to speak with Gavin. *Now.*

She strode to the front door, ignoring Juan's loud wails, Destiny and Tommy's bickering and David's sniffles. She understood the need to move all the kids to a safer location. What she didn't understand was why it was taking so long to do it.

Of course, it had only been seven minutes since Gavin walked outside. The problem was, things were breaking down. Kids getting grumpy. Virginia was getting more nervous. Cassie...well, she was about ready to raid Destiny's candy stash. The one that was probably stuffed into Destiny's backpack.

Too many emotions. That was the problem.

Too many things completely out of everyone's control.

The kids were feeling it. Virginia was. Cassie was.

If they didn't leave soon, someone was going to have a complete breakdown, and Cassie was afraid it might be her.

She swung open the door, barreled out onto the porch and straight into Gavin's arms.

"Whoa!" He grabbed her waist, his fingers warm through the thin fabric of her T-shirt. "Where are you going?"

"To find you."

"I told you that I'd be right back."

"Right back means seconds. It doesn't mean—" she glanced at her watch "—seven and a half minutes."

"Not that you were keeping track of the time or anything, right?" he asked, nudging her back inside to the crying and the whining and Virginia's wide-eyed fear.

"I was counting the nanoseconds," she replied, and he grinned, his eyes warming, his face relaxing.

Destiny's mouth dropped open.

Every bit of Virginia's fear seemed to drop away.

Cassie was too jaded to be swayed by a charming smile.

Kane had had the warmest smile she'd ever seen. He'd had the softest eyes and the prettiest words.

She'd believed every lie he'd fed her, because she'd wanted to. She'd wanted to believe in always and forever, and that her dreams were as important as his.

She grabbed the last box of Tommy's stuffed animals and took Rachel's hand. "Everyone ready?"

There was a chorus of yeses and a one very loud no.

From Tommy. Of course.

"I'm sorry, buddy, but you're outvoted. Besides, this is going to be fun," she said, hoping that she could make it that way so she wouldn't be lying. She made it a policy to be honest with the kids. Honest about their parents, their families, the likelihood that they would ever have the kind of families they all seemed to long for.

"Fun? What's fun about going into witness protection?" Virginia cried. "Do you know how often witnesses get found? Do you know the horrible kinds of deaths they—"

"You may have watched a few too many crime dramas, Virginia," Gavin cut in. "You're not actually going into witness protection. You're just staying in a safe place until we find the person who wants—"

"Us dead," Virginia moaned.

"You know what? How about we see if there are any snacks in the kitchen? Something that the kids might have when we get to our new location?" Brooke took Juan from Virginia's arms, snagged her hand and dragged her way from the group

Virginia responded, but they were already down the hall and Cassie couldn't hear what she said.

It was for the best.

She didn't want to know.

She had enough worries of her own without adding her assistant's to them.

"Ready?" Gavin took Kent and Axel by the hands. "Destiny, if you can hold on to Lila and Rachel, I think David can manage himself. What do you think, my man, want to open the door and lead the way out?" he asked, and David's posture straightened, his chin going up a couple of inches.

"Yes!" he responded.

They all walked out the door. Organized and easily as if Gavin had been around for years and knew exactly how to get everyone moving in the direction they needed to go.

That should have thrilled Cassie to pieces. She was tired, her head hurt and, quite honestly, she needed a

break from the drama. The problem was, she didn't want to like Gavin. She didn't want to trust him.

First, because he was a police offer.

Second, because he was a man.

Obviously, she had a lot of baggage she needed to unpack, but she had kids to protect, and letting a guy like Gavin weasel his way into their lives wasn't the best way to do it.

They'd had enough hurts for a lifetime.

They didn't need more.

She needed *to tell* him that.

She needed to remind him of what it felt like to get hopes up and then have them dashed again. He'd been a foster kid. He understood.

Hopefully, he'd also understand exactly why she didn't want him playing up to the kids, making friends with them, convincing them that he might just be around forever.

He wouldn't be. Couldn't be. It was too much of a commitment for most people, too much time and energy and effort for sometimes minimal results.

She didn't mention it to him as he organized two other officers, helped get car seats from the van, then ushered each small group to the appropriate car. Brooke helped Virginia into her SUV and buckled Juan into the back. The cars took off one at a time and several minutes apart.

Cassie watched impatiently from the front seat of Gavin's SUV. Rachel, Destiny and Tommy were silent in the back. Gavin was silent in the driver's seat. Cassie had the absurd urge to speak into the silence.

They were leaving their home, going to some un-known location with people who were basically strang-

ers for an unknown amount of time. She couldn't think of anything comforting to say about that, so she kept her mouth shut and didn't say anything at all.

TEN

Three days in a house that wasn't their own could have been a nightmare. Cassie had expected it to be a nightmare. So far things had gone fairly smoothly.

She cracked the last of a dozen eggs into a bowl, scrambled them up and poured them into a hot pan. Nothing fancy, but fancy wasn't what the kids wanted. They wanted home-cooked and satisfying.

A shadow moved across the window above the sink. Cassie didn't blink an eye. There'd been two Capitol K-9 officers assigned to the house since she, Virginia and the kids had arrived.

And there'd been Gavin.

He'd been there more than he'd been gone, spending nights on the couch in the living room or on the futon in the back room. The house was large, with plenty of space for all eight kids, Virginia and Cassie. It didn't seem that one more person should make it feel crowded, but every time Gavin was around, the house felt filled to the brim with people and noise and distractions.

That probably wasn't a bad thing.

Cassie hadn't been sleeping well. The kids were restless and out of sorts, and Virginia was jumping at shadows. Gavin had insisted the kids stay home from school,

and that meant homeschooling all of them. Everyone was tense and a little anxious. Including Cassie. So distraction was what they all probably needed.

The problem was, Cassie didn't want the distraction to be a guy like Gavin.

She popped four pieces of bread into the toaster and yelled for the kids to come down for breakfast. She'd have preferred to let them sleep in, because she would love to have nursed a cup of coffee on the back porch. The farmhouse was in a rural community set far back from the road. If Cassie ignored the twelve-foot high fence that surrounded the property, she could almost imagine that it was a country getaway, a pretty vacation property that she and the kids were spending time in. It was quiet there, peaceful. When the kids were asleep. When they were awake, they enjoyed the huge yard, the dirt, the fruit trees that were still bare from winter.

Footsteps sounded in the hall that opened out from the kitchen. Not the quick light footsteps of one of the kids. Heavier footsteps mixed with the soft tap of dog paws on the hardwood floor.

Gavin. She knew it before he walked into the room, felt a couple of dozen butterflies jump to life in her stomach.

"Morning," he said.

"Good morning," she replied, making herself busy buttering toast so she didn't have to look at him. He looked great in the morning, his jaw dark with stubble, his eyes still heavy from sleep.

Not that she'd noticed. Much.

"What's on the agenda for today?" he asked, pouring coffee from the carafe and standing about a foot away,

his hip resting against the edge of the counter. He was in uniform, Glory on-heel.

"Same thing we've done every day." She placed slices of toast on plates, then slid four more pieces of toast into the toaster. The eggs were ready and she divvied them up onto the plates she'd already set on the counter. "Breakfast, school, playtime, chores."

"You think you can get away for a couple of hours?"

The question was so unexpected, she turned to face him, looking straight into his gorgeous eyes. "Why?"

"The forensic sketch artist that Harland requested was able to get a red-eye out of Houston last night. He'll be in later this morning."

"He's coming out to the house?"

"No. You're going to have to go to him."

"I don't know." She could hear the kids running down the stairs, knew they'd burst into the kitchen at any moment. They were as good an excuse as any for not taking a twenty-minute ride into DC with Gavin. "The kids are still unsettled. I hate to leave them when they're not feeling comfortable."

"Not comfortable? Adam said they were outside for hours yesterday, screaming and hollering so loudly he wanted ear plugs and aspirin."

"Sorry about that." She laughed. "They *were* being obnoxiously loud. I didn't have the heart to tell them to settle down." She'd loved seeing them relaxed and having fun, so she hadn't told them to quiet down.

"And will you admit that they were plenty comfortable?" he pressed, and she had no choice but to agree. The kids were antsy, but they didn't seem unhappy, and they didn't seem scared.

"I guess so."

"We've got K-9 officers, protection dogs. Plenty of security. There's really no reason for you to stay here with them."

"Virginia is still shaky. She's jumping at shadows. I can't leave her here."

"Cassie." He sighed. "Why don't you just be honest?"

"About?" she hedged, because the kids were running down the hall, and she hoped she wouldn't have time to hear what he had to say.

"You're uncomfortable around me." He took two of the plates from the counter and set them at the table as Lila and David ran in.

"What would make you say that?" she asked, and he snorted, grabbing two more plates and sliding them down in front of Destiny and Kent.

"I don't know. Maybe the fact that you avoid me like the plague."

"No, I don't." But, he was right. She *did* try to stay out of rooms when he was in them. If he was outside she went in. If he was inside, and she could be outside, she did that too.

"You do." He helped Axel into a chair, put a plate in front of him and handed him a fork, a napkin and a sippy cup that he filled with juice. Axel never ate without a drink in his hand. It was a strange little habit that Cassie hadn't quite figured out, but Gavin had noticed.

He noticed everything about everyone. He made sure everyone had his or her favorite food, favorite DVD, favorite books. He'd brought matchbox cars for Kent, a stuffed animal for Tommy, dolls for the two younger girls. He'd brought Destiny a cookbook and a bunch of ingredients and spent time discussing the best recipe for homemade bread.

He was that kind of guy, and as far as Cassie could tell the kids were really starting to like him.

Rachel padded into the kitchen, her nightgown dragging the floor, her hair sticking up in every direction. She smiled when she saw Gavin, then walked over to Cassie for a hug.

She was a sweet little girl, but whatever she'd seen the night of Michael Jeffries's murder was still sealed tight in her head. No matter how many times Cassie asked, Rachel refused to admit that she'd seen one of the boys leave his room.

As a matter of fact, all the kids were sticking to their original stories.

"Good morning!" Virginia sashayed into the kitchen, Juan on her hip. "Looks like you've been cooking, Cassie. I thought it was my turn."

It had been, but Cassie had been awake, and she'd wanted something to occupy her mind. Otherwise, images of the gunman filled it, her heart would race, and her blood would run cold. "I was up. There was no sense in you having to get up too."

"I'll take care of lunch, then," she said as she grabbed one of the plates and sat at the table, Juan in her lap. He wasn't crying for his mother as much as he had been during the first couple of days after Rosa had died. It was good for him, but sad for the woman who'd given birth to him, loved him.

"I'm glad to hear that, Virginia," Gavin said. "If you're taking care of lunch, Cassie won't have to rush to get back."

"You're going somewhere?" Virginia asked, her gaze darting from Cassie to Gavin and back again.

"Unfortunately," Cassie muttered. "I have to go meet

with a forensic sketch artist. Gavin is going to take me into DC. Unless you'd rather I not go." If Virginia didn't want Cassie to leave, maybe Gavin would bring the sketch artist out to them.

"Why wouldn't I want you to go?" Virginia looked genuinely puzzled.

"Things have been a little crazy lately. I don't want to leave you here with the kids if you're not feeling safe and secure."

"It would be hard not to feel safe," Virginia said. "There's a twelve-foot fence surrounding the property, guard dogs and police officers."

"I was hoping you'd feel that way," Gavin said, and Virginia blushed. "I think that settles it, Cassie. You're free to come to DC with me."

"Wonderful," she replied.

"Try not to sound too enthusiastic." He filled her coffee cup, opened the fridge and took out the creamer, then poured a splash into the coffee. If he scooped a spoonful of sugar in...

He did, stirring it around three times like she always did.

"Here you go." He handed it to her, and she took a sip. Strong and just a little sweet. Kind of like the man who'd poured it for her.

She frowned, staring into her coffee cup. "Thanks. What time do you want to leave?"

"How long will it take you to get ready?"

"Maybe thirty minutes." She could actually do it more quickly, but Tommy hadn't come down for breakfast, and she had a feeling she was in for a struggle with him. He'd been grumpy and quiet since they'd left All Our Kids. It worried her, but the more she pushed him

to open up to her, the more he sank into himself and refused to communicate. "I've got to wake Tommy up. Then, we can leave."

"I can do that for you," Virginia offered.

"It's okay. I have to go upstairs for my purse, anyway. Be back in a few minutes." She hurried out of the room, anxious to get her things and go, to get the trip over with. She felt nervous about the sketch artist, afraid that she wouldn't be able to describe the person she'd seen well enough for the description to be translated into a drawing.

She was nervous about Gavin, too. About spending more time with him, about seeing things in him that she didn't want to see. Good things. Admirable things.

She scowled, taking the stairs two at a time. There were five bedrooms upstairs. The girls shared one, the boys shared one. She and Virginia had their own, and Juan had the tiny room at the end of the hall.

The door to the boys' room was closed, and Cassie knocked, waited a moment and opened the door.

"Tommy—" she began, but the room was empty. No one on either set of bunk beds. No one under them. She checked the closet. Empty.

Her heart thumped painfully as she looked in the girls' room, Juan's room, Virginia's room. "Tommy!" she called.

Had he gone outside?

She ran back downstairs. Gavin and Glory were waiting at the front door.

"Everything okay?" Gavin asked.

"I can't find Tommy."

He frowned. "Where'd you look?"

"Every room upstairs. He's not there."

"You looked under beds?"

"Yes."

"Closets?"

"Gavin," she snapped, impatient with the questions, terrified that Tommy had run away. "I looked. I didn't find him." She sidled past him and opened the small coat closet that was on the wall next to the front door. Tommy's coat still hung there with the others. His shoes were on the little shoe rack beneath the coats.

She unlocked the door, would have walked outside, but Gavin touched her shoulder. "Do you really think he could have gone outside?"

"I—"

"We've got a state-of-the-art security system, Cassie, and it's on all night every night. If he opened a door or window, the alarm would have gone off. If he'd walked outside, Adam or Nicholas would have seen him."

"Maybe. Tommy is wily."

"Not wily enough to get past a Doberman pinscher or a Rottweiler." His hand slid from her shoulder down her arm, rested on her wrist. "Did you forget Ace and Max were out there?"

She had, and remembering made her legs weak with relief. "Right. I forgot." She let out a shaky laugh. "So, he's in the house somewhere. I'd better search upstairs a little more carefully."

"You could." He snagged Tommy's jacket from the closet without having to ask which one it was. "Or Glory could."

"I forgot about that, too. I guess Virginia is rubbing off on me. I panicked before I thought."

"You aren't even close to the kind of person who panics before she thinks." He held the jacket out, let-

ting Glory sniff the fabric. Her ears perked up, her dark brown eyes alert and interested.

"Go!" he commanded. "Find."

Whether she smelled Tommy or heard him, Cassie didn't know, but the shepherd didn't hesitate. She padded up the stairs, stuck her head in the boys' room, reconsidered and walked farther down the hall.

She nosed Cassie's closed bedroom door, scratching at the wood. "Did you check in here?" Gavin asked as he opened the door.

"No. The kids know better than to go in my room."

"And, they follow the rules all the time, huh?" He walked into the room behind Glory, and Cassie followed. Aside from Juan's room, it was the smallest. Ten by ten with a twin bed, a small dresser and one window that looked out over the backyard.

Glory padded to the closet, scratched the door and sat.

"Looks like we've found our mark," Gavin said quietly.

Cassie opened the door. She'd only brought jeans, T-shirts, a dress, a couple of skirts and blouses, two pair of shoes, so there wasn't much in the closet. Or shouldn't have been. Tommy was there, huddled on the floor with six of his stuffed animals. He'd been crying, his face streaked with tears, his cheeks red.

She didn't try to get him to come out, just crawled in beside him and put an arm around his stiff shoulders. "Buddy, what in the world are you doing in here?"

"Nothing." He sniffed, wiping at his nose with the sleeve of his superhero pajamas.

"Are you sad because we had to leave the other house?" she suggested. Tommy didn't usually cry, and seeing him so upset broke her heart.

He shook his head, pulled his knees up to his chin and laid his cheek against them.

"Are you sure?"

He didn't respond, so she did what she'd learned to do with kids like him. She didn't say anything, just sat beside him and waited.

Gavin had been forced to learn the fine art of patience years ago, but it still didn't come easily to him. That was a shame, seeing as how he was currently spending almost all of his time in a house filled to the brim with kids. None of whom were eager to cooperate with him.

Case in point—Tommy.

The kid knew something, Gavin was almost certain of it.

But, no matter how many times Gavin asked, no matter how many ways he asked, he got nothing from him.

He glanced at his watch, the silence in the room deafening. Neither Cassie nor Tommy seemed eager to break it. Any other day, that would have been fine, but Gavin was on a tight timeline. He was supposed to have Cassie at headquarters within the hour. The forensic sketch artist had limited time in DC, and if they missed the window of opportunity, Harland's efforts to get the guy in would have been wasted.

He cleared his throat, hoping Cassie would get the hint and try to move things along.

She shot him a hard look, her eyes bright but deeply shadowed. She hadn't been sleeping well. He'd heard the floor creaking above his head as she'd paced her room, heard her move from one room to the next, checking on kids. He'd thought about walking up the stairs and offering her a cup of coffee, a glass of milk, a willing ear.

But that had seemed like a bad idea.

He needed to keep his distance.

That's what his job required. It was also what his life required. He didn't have anything to offer a woman like Cassie. She was all about family and connection, about sitting down to dinner every night with eight kids, hearing every minute detail of each child's day. She was about playing tag in the backyard, chasing preteens and toddlers until everyone was squealing and laughing.

Tommy shifted, and Gavin hoped the kid was finally going to speak.

"I'm hungry," he said, and Cassie sighed.

"That's all you have to say after coming in my room and hiding in my closet?"

"It's not your room. It's his room." Tommy jabbed his finger in Gavin's direction. "'Cause this is his house."

"It's not my house, champ," he corrected. "It belongs to the people I work for."

Tommy shrugged, shuffling out of the closet on his knees, all his stuffed animals clutched in his arms. "It's still not Cassie's."

"That doesn't mean you get to invade my privacy, Tommy," Cassie responded calmly. In the three days she and the kids had been at the safe house, Gavin had never seen her come even close to losing her cool with any of them. She had more patience than anyone Gavin had ever known.

"I'm sorry, Cassie. I just didn't want the bad man to get me," Tommy whispered, and everything inside Gavin went still and calm and careful. This was what he'd wanted to talk about. This was what he'd waited three days to hear.

"What bad man?" Cassie asked, crawling out of the

closet behind him. She could have been asking about the color of the sky or the warmth of the sun for all the excitement in her voice. What wasn't there was in her eyes. Gavin could see it in the sharpness of her gaze as she crouched in front of Tommy, put a hand on his shoulder.

"The one with the gun," he said, and Cassie's gaze shifted to Gavin. He knew that she felt what he did. This could be it. The moment when Tommy admitted that he'd been out of the house, been to Harland's place, seen something that he shouldn't have seen.

"You saw him?" Cassie asked quietly. "At Congressman Jeffries's house?"

Tommy hesitated, then shook his head violently. "No! I told you no! I didn't see nothing!"

He jerked away from Cassie, ran down the stairs, his feet pounding on the wood.

She didn't get up, didn't move, and Gavin thought he saw a little piece of her heart break right in front of his eyes.

He took her hand, tugged her to her feet. "It's okay," he said, because he thought she needed to hear it.

"Not really." She rubbed the back of her neck, her hair loose for a change. No high ponytail or messy bun, the glossy strands fell to the center of her back and clung to her neck and her shoulder. "I've worked so hard to get Tommy to open up to me. Now we're back at square one, doing the same things we were doing when he first came to me."

"Isn't that the way it always is?" It was the way it had been with him. Two steps forward. One step back. Repeating the same bad patterns of behavior over and over again, always hoping to get a different result. It had taken time and maturity to work through that, to figure

out a way to make healthy choices that would lead him in the right direction.

He would have told her that, but they were running late. The sketch artist was waiting with Margaret and all the members of Capitol K-9 who weren't on duty. So far, they had plenty of questions and no answers. The search warrant for Erin's apartment had finally come through, but a thorough search of the residence had revealed nothing. No hint as to where she'd gone, why she'd gone. No hidden diary revealing some secret hatred of Michael, some reason why she might want him dead.

They were exactly where they'd been four days ago—two dead, two wounded, Cassie the only—talking—witness who'd seen a face, eyes, hair color.

"It is, but that doesn't make it easier," she said, her voice breaking on the last word, and suddenly the need to leave wasn't quite as compelling.

"He'll come around."

"Maybe." She turned away, and he thought she might be fighting tears. If so, it would be the first hint of them he'd seen. She came off as strong, almost invincible, but looking at her there—standing with her face to the sunlight that streamed through her window, her body encased in baggy jeans and an oversize T-shirt, she looked vulnerable and alone

"Cassie." He touched her shoulder, urging her around so they were face-to-face. The cut on her forehead had scabbed over, her thick bangs nearly covering it. She had a bruise on her jaw, shadows under her eyes, but she met his eyes without hesitation, looked straight at him in a way most people didn't. "He will come around, because of you."

"Despite me, you mean?"

"I mean what I said. Tommy needs you in his life. You'll be the difference that he remembers when he's my age."

"Who was yours?" she asked, grabbing an oversize sweatshirt from one of the drawers and pulling it on over her T-shirt, her hair trapped beneath the collar.

He freed it, unconsciously doing what he'd done for Helena. Only Cassie's hair was softer. Not the processed blond strands that Helena had teased and sprayed. It was natural, silky, the strands sliding along his fingers and his wrists.

She blushed, and he felt a moment of such pure tenderness, he had to step back, put a little space between them. "The difference I remember?" he responded, his voice a little gruffer than he'd intended. "Mrs. Simons. She was housemother at All Our Kids when I arrived. That woman knew how to get what she wanted."

"What did she want?" she asked as she shoved her feet into sneakers, her back to him again, her hair falling in a long wave of silken strands down her back.

"To watch me graduate from high school, see me go to college, cheer for me when I got my degree."

"Did she?" She turned, the sunlight from the window glinting in her hair and splashing across her pale cheeks. It wasn't an idle question. He could see that in her eyes, see just how much she wanted to know the answer.

"Cassie," he said, hooking his arm through hers and leading her to the door because they *were* on a time crunch. "Mrs. Simons hounded me all the way through high school graduation, helped me find scholarship money for college, cheered louder than anyone in the crowd when I got my degree. Now she's living in Florida,

waiting for me to get married so she can buy a mother-of-the-groom dress."

"Is she really?"

"As sure as I'm standing here telling you the story, she is." They reached the top of the steps, and she jogged down ahead of him. The woman had more energy than any three people Gavin knew.

He guessed she needed that and more to deal with her crew.

She stopped at the door, tugged her hair into a messy bun. Several strands escaped, but she didn't seem to care. "Are you going to let her?"

"Let her what?" he asked.

"Wear the mother-of-the-groom dress?"

"If I ever get married, she'll not only be wearing the dress, but she'll be dancing the mother-and-son dance with me." Of course, he'd told Mrs. Simons there was no chance of him getting married, no reason for her to put away money for a plane trip or a fancy dress. She'd laughed, and told him that everything would happen according to God's plan and in His time.

Gavin believed that, he just didn't believe that God's plan included all the things his foster mother wanted for him.

"I hope that's me one day," Cassie said wistfully. "Dancing with David or Tommy or Kent or Axel. Or maybe standing in as mother for one of the girls. Of course, I have to make sure they all get to adulthood before that happens. I'll go tell Virginia we're leaving. I'll be right back."

She jogged down the hall, her baggy jeans skimming the floor. From the back, she looked like a kid. In every other way, she was a woman.

Gavin had noticed. More than once.

It would probably be best if he stopped, but when it came to Cassie, he had a difficult time pretending not to see what was there.

His cell phone rang, and he answered, his gaze still focused on the hallway that Cassie had just walked down.

"Gavin here."

"It's Isaac. I got a call from the DC police. Rosa Gomez has a sister. Name's Lana Gomez."

"They finally located her?" he asked, the sound of Cassie's voice drifting out from the kitchen.

"Yes. The two were estranged, and she hadn't spoken to her in a while."

"Has she been interviewed?"

"Yes, and she's agreed to speak with us. I've got her scheduled for tomorrow night. Seven o'clock. Would have made it earlier, but she works. Is the time okay for you?" Isaac asked. He wasn't the kind of officer who waited around for instructions. He assessed situations, figured out what needed to be done and did it.

"I'll make sure it is." He was interested to see what Lana Gomez had to say. There had to be a story behind her estrangement from her sister, a reason why the two hadn't been on speaking terms.

Whether or not that had anything to do with Rosa's death remained to be seen. He said goodbye and tucked the phone back in his pocket as Cassie hurried toward him.

ELEVEN

Traffic on the beltway was terrible, cars backed up bumper to bumper, trucks inching along the road. Gavin didn't seem bothered by the delay. His hands were loose on the steering wheel, his body relaxed. He kept up an easy conversation, asking about each of the kids, about Virginia, about how Cassie had gotten the job of housemother.

She answered, but she felt tense, each slow mile making her more anxious. She'd left the kids on a few occasions, but never when they'd been upset or scared.

Today, Tommy had been both.

He'd also been angry, and Cassie wasn't sure why. Maybe because he'd wanted her to stay. Whatever the case, he'd looked almost exactly like he'd looked the day he'd arrived at All Our Kids—irate, truculent, unapproachable.

"I've lost you to something," Gavin said as he finally exited the beltway and headed into the heart of DC. "Want to tell me what?"

"No." She didn't talk to many people about the kids. Sure, she spoke with their counselors, their teachers, their Sunday school teachers. She and Virginia talked, but Cassie didn't share details about the kids with her

friends. They didn't understand. Not how deep the kids' wounds went. They said they did. They gave lip service to sympathy, but empathy was difficult to come by when a kid who was visiting stole a favorite knickknack or kicked a beloved pet.

"Then, maybe I should take a wild guess."

"Don't put yourself to too much trouble. It's not that important."

He laughed. "No trouble at all. Here's the way I see it. You're thinking about Tommy. You're thinking that you shouldn't have left him. You're thinking that everything you've worked hard to accomplish has been undone by circumstances that are beyond your control."

"Something like that," she admitted.

"He'll be fine," Gavin assured her. "Kids usually are."

"That's not true, and you know it. We like to say that, because it makes us feel better, but trauma is just as difficult on kids as it is on adults."

"I didn't say it wasn't, Cassie. I said they're usually fine. The thing about kids is that they still have hope. No matter how bad the situation, they always think that something better might be right around the corner." He turned left, heading down a narrow side street. She knew the area. They were close to the White House and Capitol Hill. Not far from the heartbeat of the federal government. "Adults know better. They know that the next corner could hide blessings or misery, so they're not as likely to be optimistic during difficult circumstances."

"Some of us are," she responded. At least Cassie tried to be. It could be difficult. Sometimes, she'd take a dozen steps forward with a kid and find herself back at the beginning again.

"Then why are you worried about Tommy?"

"Because, there's no one else to do it?"

"There's God. Isn't that enough?"

"You know it is," she muttered.

"Then stop worrying and start trusting."

"It's not that easy."

"It is if you want it to be." He turned down a narrow alley that opened up onto a quiet street.

Maybe he was right.

Maybe it was as easy as that.

She still wanted to be back at the safe house with Tommy.

"You've got your seat belt on, right?" Gavin asked suddenly.

"Yes. Wh—"

He accelerated, swerving around a slow-moving truck, taking a sharp turn onto another side street. Glory let out a quiet bark and shifted position in her crate. Like Cassie, she must be sensing trouble.

"What's going on?" Cassie asked, shifting in her seat and trying to see out the back window.

"Maybe nothing," he said.

"Or maybe what?"

"Or maybe someone is following us," he replied, glancing in the rearview mirror and frowning.

Maybe or for sure? she wanted to ask, but the words stuck in her throat. There were several vehicles behind them. A sporty Mazda. An old station wagon. A Jeep. A white panel van. A pickup truck. None of them seemed any more suspicious than another.

"Which one?" she whispered as if whoever was following could hear. She cleared her throat, tried again. "Which one?"

"The white van. It's been behind us since we entered the city limits."

"There are vans just like it all over the city," she said. More to reassure herself than to sway Gavin.

"Not many of them would take that alley I just went through. It's narrow and not easy to turn into." He used his radio to call in their location and ask for backup.

That should have been reassuring, but it only made Cassie more nervous.

"How far are we from your office?"

"Not far." He took another quick turn, glanced in the rearview mirror and frowned. "Looks like he's gone."

"You don't seem happy about it." Cassie was thrilled. She'd been envisioning a car chase through the city, jumping curbs and doing U-turns into oncoming traffic.

"I'm not happy about anything that's happened the past few days." He pulled up to a gate and punched a number into a small panel. "I'm especially not happy that you and your kids are involved."

"I'm not all that excited about it, either."

"You know we're going to have to grill Tommy a little harder, right? Ask Rachel a few more questions?" The gate swung open, and he pulled through. Cassie tried not to notice the armed guard sitting in a booth a few feet away.

"I've been trying to get them both to open up."

"Trying isn't working for anyone, Cassie. We've got to get the truth out of them."

"I know."

"Good. Does tonight work for you? We can go back to the house, bring the kids some ice cream or something—"

"How about we skip the sugar? It took the kids an

hour longer than usual to fall asleep after the dough-nut incident."

"I was trying to get the kids to warm up to me."

"Then play a game of tag with them. Or show them some of Glory's cool moves."

Glory barked in response to her name, and Gavin smiled.

"Glory likes that idea, so I might try it. Can I bribe *you* with sugar?" He parked the SUV near the entrance of a two-story brick building. A few other cars dotted the small parking lot. Nothing too impressive, but there were security cameras mounted to the exterior walls.

"Bribe me to what?" she asked, shifting her gaze from the building to Gavin.

Big mistake.

There was plenty of space between them. An entire console of air, but he had the bluest eyes she'd ever seen. The warmest smile. She'd looked at him plenty of times while he'd been helping at the house or schmoozing at some gala event for All Our Kids, but she'd never really *seen* him.

"I need you to let me deal with Tommy," he said. "Let me be the one to talk to him, try to get him to open up about what he saw."

"*If* he saw anything. It's possible—"

"Don't kid yourself, Cassie," he said, his gaze hard, his tone firm. "He saw something. He's scared to death. You saw the way he acted when Harland was asking questions, the way he's acted every time someone brings up the night of the murder."

He was right.

"I—"

"Trust me on this, okay?" He touched her hand, his

fingers sliding along her knuckles before they drifted away. "I'm not going to do anything to traumatize him further, but I can't have my hands tied. I've got to do my job."

"Of course you do," she said, her head filling with a dozen years' worth of police officers saying the same thing as they ransacked her room, looking for drugs.

"What's that supposed to mean?"

"You know where I grew up, Gavin?" she asked. "I grew up in the worst area of DC in the ugliest little house God ever allowed to exist. There was mold growing on the ceilings and water dripped through the roof when it rained. My grandmother grew pot in little planters on the back deck and she sold just about every prescription painkiller you can imagine."

"I'm sorry, Cassie. No kid should live like that."

"True, but that's not why I'm telling you about it. The house was ugly, my grandmother was neglectful at best and abusive at worst, but I had a room, a bed, a bookshelf filled with library books and schoolbooks. A couple of times a month, some druggie would decide he'd been cheated and call in information to the police. They'd arrive in the middle of the night or early in the morning, banging on the door. I'd hear them, but I'd always stay in bed with the covers over my head, hoping they'd just leave me alone. They never did. They always came and dragged me out of bed, made me stand in the hall while they tore my room apart. Sometimes, I'd cry. Sometimes I wouldn't, but I always heard the same either way— 'Sorry, kid, but I've got to do my job.'" She grabbed the door handle, shoved the door open, and tumbled out into the parking lot.

She didn't wait for Gavin, didn't want to hear what-

ever excuses he'd offer. She'd grown up. She understood. But she wasn't going to let her kids feel the same sense of helplessness she'd felt. Not if she could help it.

She reached the door of the building, tried to open it. Locked. Gavin was getting Glory out of the SUV. He'd have the code or the key or whatever was needed to open the door.

But she didn't want to look in his eyes again, didn't want to stand close and inhale his masculine scent. Didn't want to think that he was different from other guys she'd known, that he was different from Kane.

She pivoted to the right and headed for the corner of the building. A place like this didn't only have one door. She'd find another way in, and then she was going to find the nearest restroom and splash her face with icy water. Fatigue was messing with her head. She needed it to be un-messed with. Otherwise, she might find herself wanting things she couldn't have, believing in stuff that was never going to happen.

She wasn't going to get into the building, but Cassie obviously didn't know it. Gavin hooked Glory to her lead and followed Cassie as she checked the side entrance and then the rear entrance. She was heading around to the east side of the building, when he snagged the back of her sweatshirt and pulled her to a stop.

"They're all locked," he said. "So, how about you stop wasting time looking for one that will open?"

"You could have told me that two doors ago," she said, shoving her hands into the front pocket of her sweatshirt and sighing.

"I thought you might need to walk off some steam."

"I wasn't mad."

"I know." He nudged her back to the west-side entrance and used his key to open it. His office was on the second floor. Since the stairs were closer than the elevator, he led her there. "That doesn't mean you don't need to walk off some steam."

"You're afraid I'm too upset to give the sketch artist what he needs," she accused.

He couldn't deny it.

He needed her description to be clear and precise, but he needed her to be okay, too. She might not understand that. Not after spending her childhood being on the wrong end of enthusiastic law enforcement. He'd like her to understand it, though.

"*Are* you too upset to do this?" he countered as they reached the second story. A hall stretched out to either side of the stairwell. His office was to the left, and he could see that the door was open.

Margaret had probably brought the sketch artist in.

"What if I said yes?"

"Then I'd ask if I could get you a cup of coffee and give you a minute to think about how important this is. Not just to my case, but to you and the kids."

"I don't need a reminder, but I wouldn't mind having a cup of coffee." She smiled, but there wasn't any energy in it, no sparkle of amusement in her eyes. She looked exhausted, and he had a moment of doubt, a moment when he wondered if he should take her back down to the SUV and drive her back to the safe house.

"Gavin!" Margaret Meyer stepped out of Gavin's office and hurried toward them, her heels clicking on the tile floor. Short with a petite build and striking blue eyes, she'd built Capitol K-9 from the ground up. "Glad you finally made it. Pretty terrible traffic today, huh?"

"Worse than usual. Is the sketch artist here?"

"Yes. Congressman Jeffries is with him." Margaret's gaze shifted to Cassie, and she smiled. "You're Cassie Danvers. I think we've met at one of Harland's parties."

"I think we have," Cassie agreed. "It's nice to see you again."

"Nicer if it weren't under these circumstances, right?" Margaret took her arm as if they were old friends and walked her into the office.

Gavin followed, Glory on heel beside him. She knew the building, the office, the people, and her body was relaxed, her tail wagging happily.

Harland was standing near the window, a dark-haired man beside him. An inch shorter than the congressman, he wore black slacks and a dress shirt unbuttoned at the collar. There was no doubt he was the sketch artist. He had a pencil in one hand and a cup of coffee in the other.

"Cassie," Harland said, crossing the room and taking her hand. He looked thinner, the hollows beneath his cheekbones more pronounced. "I'm glad you were up to this. I was worried that with all the stress, you might not feel ready to provide a description."

"I'd do anything to help the police find Michael's..." She shook her head. "I don't want to leave the kids for too long, though."

"We can get started, then," the sketch artist said. "I'm Westland Granger, by the way. You can call me West. Everyone else does. Mind if I use your desk to get set up?" He lifted an oversize portfolio from the floor and pulled a large sketch pad from it. "We'll start with a good old-fashioned pencil sketch. I may switch to my computer system later."

He sat in a chair and pushed a few of Gavin's things

to the edge of the desk. "Also," he continued. "Unless you're all opposed to it, I prefer to work alone with the witness. Too many people in the space while I'm working is distracting."

"I'm opposed," Gavin said.

Margaret frowned. "On what grounds?"

"We don't know who's responsible for Michael's death. We don't know if it's one person or several."

"You can't think I had anything to do with it." West set his pad on the table and smoothed one of the pages. "I was a thousand miles away."

"People can call the shots from ten thousand miles away, if they have the money and know-how to do it."

"I don't have, either. Even if I did, why would I?" West didn't seem bothered by Gavin's comment. "I've got nothing to gain."

"He also has top secret clearance and has had enough background checks in his life for me to feel pretty certain he's a good guy," Harland cut in. "I know you're worried, but I think your worry is misplaced."

Maybe so. Probably so. They were in one of the most secure buildings in DC. There were cameras and monitors in every office. There was no way for someone to get in or out without being seen.

"How about Cassie decides? Are you going to be okay here by yourself?" he asked, ignoring Harland's hard look and Margaret's frown. They both knew him well enough to know he was going to do this the way it made sense to him. If Cassie didn't want to be left alone with the sketch artist, she wouldn't be. And he didn't care who said otherwise.

Cassie eyed West thoughtfully, then nodded. "I think I can take him down if I have to."

West laughed at that, smoothing his hand over the paper again. "I hear you wrangle eight kids for a living. I'd say you could take me down easy."

"That's settled, then. How about the three of us grab some coffee? I've got a fresh pot in my office," Margaret offered, leading Harland into the hall.

"That leaves you," West prodded, motioning for Gavin to go.

He knew he wasn't being reasonable. He knew Cassie would be safe in his office. But he didn't want to leave her there.

He met her eyes, and she smiled, gave a little nod that was supposed to make him feel better about going.

It didn't.

Not because she was a key witness to a crime he was trying to solve. Not because he had to keep her safe so she could testify at a trial if there ever was one.

Those things mattered, but Cassie mattered more.

He wanted to keep her safe because she deserved it. He wanted to protect her because he couldn't imagine the world without her in it.

He frowned, leading Glory out of his office and down the hall to Margaret's corner office. Though her main office was at the White House, she kept one at K-9 Headquarters, too. Gavin liked that about her. That she was eager to stay connected with the team, to work with the group she'd so carefully put together only added to the respect the group had for her. When he stepped through the open doorway, he found Margaret alone, leaning toward her computer screen, a frown carving deep lines into her face.

She didn't look up as he dropped into a chair.

"Where's Harland?"

"He realized he had a checkup with his doctor and left. Which is good. I wanted to speak with you in private."

"What's up?" he asked.

She studied her computer screen, then typed something.

He waited her out. Margaret was never rude, but she was always focused. She worked harder than anyone Gavin had ever met, and she expected the same dedication from her team.

Finally, she leaned back, eyeing him from across the table. "You seem to be growing fond of Cassie."

There was no sense denying it. "And?"

"It's not going to interfere with the job, is it?"

"You don't know me very well if you think that's even a possibility."

"I *do* know you well. That's why I'm letting you decide if you want to keep this case or hand it over to someone else."

"I've got no reason to hand it over."

"That's what I wanted to hear." She smiled. "You know that we've got a meeting with Rosa Gomez's sister tomorrow, right? I was thinking that Cassie could be there. Tell her about Juan's routine. What he likes to eat. When he sleeps. That sort of thing. We all want this transition to be as easy as possible for him and for her."

He nodded. "That shouldn't be a problem."

"And, hopefully, you'll bring a few more answers. Any change in the kids' stories?"

"They're sticking to their guns, refusing to admit anything."

"You don't think they're telling the truth?"

"No. I'm pretty certain that one of the boys was at Harland's house. Getting him to admit it is the problem."

"Keep trying." She glanced at her watch and frowned. "I've got a meeting with White House security in ten. Let me know if I can do anything to help move this case along. I liked Michael. He was a good kid. He deserved better."

She walked out of the office, and Gavin was left with his coffee and his thoughts. The coffee was good. The thoughts weren't.

Every day that passed without a suspect in custody was a day that justice hadn't been done. He rose in the morning thinking about that, went to bed at night with it on his mind. He tried to keep his focus on the evidence and the leads, but it was hard.

Glory whined, pacing to the door and looking out into the hall.

"You hear one of your buddies, girl?" He scratched behind her ears, rubbed the scruff of her neck. She was a social dog, a hard worker who loved people and other animals. She got along with cats, birds and kids, too. When she needed to be on guard, though, when she needed to protect, she could. That was one of the things that made her a great partner.

He poured coffee into a second cup, called for Glory to heel. He wasn't supposed to sit in his office while West worked, but he'd promised Cassie coffee, and he was going to bring it to her. It would give him a chance to check in, make sure that she really was doing okay.

Then, he'd get on the phone, see if the DC police had located the car that had nearly run him down a few days ago, see if they'd found Erin's vehicle. There were plenty of loose ends that needed to be tied up, plenty of

leads that needed to be followed. It was going to take time. Maybe a lot of it. In the end, Gavin and Capitol K-9 would find the person who'd killed Michael. When they did, they'd make sure he paid.

TWELVE

The sketch was spot-on.

It looked so much like the guy who'd been on her back porch that Cassie shuddered as she handed it back to West. "That looks just like him."

"That's what I try to do. Hopefully, we can use this in the face recognition program the FBI has. I'll give this to Margaret. She can have someone run it through the database. It may take minutes or days to spit out some possibilities. If it gives you any at all. If the guy is a career criminal, he'll be in there. If not..." He shrugged.

"If not, I guess we aren't any worse off than we were before." She took a sip from the cup of coffee Gavin had brought her. Stone-cold, it went down like a bitter pill, catching in her throat and making her long for a glass of water.

"True. I like my sketches to do some good, though. You know? Get the bad guys, put them behind bars. The job is more satisfying that way." He stood and stretched, rubbing the back of his neck. "Any idea where Margaret or Harland went? I need to clear this with them and hit the road. I have a meeting in Jacksonville in the morning."

"I can go look for them." She needed to stretch, too.

The process had taken nearly two hours, and her muscles felt tense from sitting for so long.

"Nah. Sit tight. I'll call Harland." He walked out of the room, and she was left by herself, the sketch of the man who'd tried to kill her sitting on the desk.

The face was good, the contours of it nearly perfect. It was the eyes, though, that looked the most like her attacker's—cold and dead. Expressionless.

She wanted to turn the sketch over so she didn't have to see it. West had sprayed it with something to hold the pencil in place, but she was still afraid she'd smudge it.

She took another sip of the coffee. Her brain was sluggish, her thinking slow. She knew one thing, though. She had to get Tommy and Rachel to talk about what had happened the night Michael was murdered.

Her stomach growled, and she opened her purse. She had eight kids who were always hungry. She should have something in there. A candy bar, a protein bar, a couple pieces of gum. She'd eat crumbs if she could locate a couple.

Footsteps tapped on the floor outside the office, and Gavin appeared, Glory at his side.

"Looking for something?" he asked, his gaze on the bag that was sitting in her lap.

"Food, but I think Destiny cleaned me out." She closed the bag and met Gavin's bright blue eyes. "West finished the sketch."

"I saw him heading toward Margaret's office. How'd it go?" he asked.

"The image is perfect." She gestured to the sketch, and he lifted it carefully, studying it for a few seconds.

"Guy looks about as cold as ice."

"That's how he looked the night Michael was killed."

She walked to the window that faced the parking lot. There wasn't a whole lot to see—a few cars, the road beyond the fenced lot, a few tall buildings that she knew were toward the center of the city. She kept looking, anyway. It was better than staring at the face of the man who'd be happy if she and her kids were dead.

"You're upset by this sketch, huh?"

"Not really. It's just a good reminder that I need to get the kids talking. As soon as I get back to the safe house, I'm going to talk to Rachel and Tommy."

"I thought we agreed that I'd work with Tommy."

"We didn't agree." She turned and realized that he was right behind her, their bodies as close as a breath. She backed up, bumping into the windowsill.

"Then, how about we agree now?"

"How about you let me give it another shot before we do?" she responded, trying to ease out from between Gavin and the window, move away from him and the heady scent of outdoors and man that clung to him.

"You can't keep running away, Cassie," he said, putting a hand on her shoulder and holding her in place.

"I'm not running away. I'm just…" *Putting a little distance between us? Getting some air? Clearing my head so I can think again?* None of them seemed like the right thing to say, but all of them were the truth.

"You're running because you're afraid that I'm not going to listen to what you have to say. You're afraid I'm going to take over your life, destroy the peace that you have with the kids."

Maybe. Probably. She didn't want to admit it, though. It seemed almost childish to want to cling so hard to control. "I just don't want the kids hurt."

"Then you're going to have to let me and my team protect them."

"That's what I'm doing. That's why we're in the safe house."

"You're in the safe house, but you're tying my hands."

"I'm not."

"You are," he said calmly, not a hint of irritation or frustration in his voice. "I need to talk to Tommy. I need to push him to give me some real answers, some truthful ones. I understand your reluctance, but you have to understand my position."

She did. That was the problem.

She glanced at the desk, the face of the man who'd tried to kill her, who might have killed Michael Jeffries. "All right. You can talk to Tommy."

"Alone?" he pressed.

"Yes," she snapped. "Alone."

"No need to be a sore loser," he said mildly.

"I'm not a sore loser," she replied. "I'm a hungry one. I didn't eat breakfast. I didn't eat lunch, and my coffee was cold." Her voice wobbled, and she had the insane urge to cry. It was completely out of proportion to the situation. She knew it, but she was tired, hungry, frustrated.

"You're tired," he said, as if he'd read her thoughts. "That's the problem. You need to get some food and get some sleep." His hand drifted from her shoulder to her nape, his fingers kneading the tense muscles in her neck. She wanted to lean closer. "We can talk after that."

"I thought we already talked."

"We talked about the case, about Tommy, about your empty stomach. We didn't talk about you." His thumb brushed against the tender flesh behind her ear, swept

along her jaw. "I want to hear more about your grand-mother and your childhood."

"It's a boring story." She ducked away from his arm and took a couple of quick steps across the room.

"Nothing about you is boring," he responded, and she blushed.

"Pretty words, but I'd rather have a hot meal."

"I can arrange for that, too," he said, his hand on her lower spine as he walked her into the hallway. The air was cooler there, their footsteps echoing on the tile floor. The sound didn't cover the thundering pulse of blood in her ears.

"What are you doing, Gavin?" she asked, because that was the kind of person she was. She didn't wait around hoping to figure things out. She asked, got answers, for-mulated plans, implemented them. She'd learned to take care of herself a long time ago, and then she'd learned to take care of others. What she'd never learned was how to let other people take care of her.

"Getting you some food, bringing you back to your kids."

"That's not what I mean."

"Isn't it?" They reached the staircase, and he walked down in front of her, Glory at his side. Dog and cop made a good-looking pair, a great team, and she thought that if anyone could make sure the kids stayed safe, it was the two of them.

"What's with the offers of bringing me food? What's with the compliments? I've already told you everything I can about the guy who shot Officer—"

"Do you really think that's the kind of person I am?" He cut her off as he opened the door at the bottom of the

stairs. Watery sunlight streamed into the stairwell. "The kind who does things so he can get things?"

"No," she responded honestly as she walked outside. She didn't think that was how he was. He seemed more like the kind of guy who took care of everyone in his life. "And I'm sorry if you thought I was implying it. I'm… just not used to having someone looking out for me."

"Maybe it's something you can get used to, then, because I always look out for the people in my life." He unlocked the SUV, holding the door as she slid into the passenger seat.

I'm not in your life, she almost said, but he closed the door, led Glory around to the back, and she let it drop.

The fact was, she *was* in his life.

The other fact was, she didn't really mind having him look after her.

She wasn't sure if she should be worried about that, and she was too tired to think about what it meant, so she laid her head back against the seat, closed her eyes, tried to let the sunlight and the rumble of the engine and the soft sound of Gavin on his cell phone fade away.

The problem was, every time the world faded, *his* face appeared—blond hair and dead eyes.

She jerked upright, her heart thundering, her body cold with fear. She'd been trying hard not to let the kids know how afraid she was. She'd hidden the truth from Virginia, too. Admitting the depth of her terror wasn't going to help anyone. It certainly wasn't going to help the kids sleep better at night.

"Cold?" Gavin asked as he punched a code into the closed gate, waiting while it slid open.

"A little," she said, even though she felt a bone-deep chill that she didn't think she'd ever be able to shake.

"Here." He slid out of his jacket and tucked it around her upper body, surrounding her in warmth and with his masculine scent.

She could have pushed the jacket away, told him that she didn't need it, but she just burrowed in deeper, closing her eyes again. This time, the image of the man with the cold dead eyes didn't fill her head. This time, all she could see was Gavin's face, his vivid blue eyes, his smile.

They were being followed.

Gavin glanced in the rearview mirror, spotted the white panel van six cars back and hanging there. He slowed down, pulling into the right lane and letting a couple of dozen cars pass. The van stayed where it was, puttering along at Gavin's pace.

He called in his location, keeping his voice low, hoping not to wake Cassie. Until he knew they were in imminent danger, there was no sense in alarming her.

He exited the beltway well before he needed to.

If the guy in the van was on a fact-finding mission, he wasn't going to find anything other than trouble. The DC police didn't have jurisdiction in Maryland, so he called his location in to the state police, asking for a patrol car to respond.

Hopefully, they'd be there sooner rather than later.

He turned off the main highway, speeding through a small community and out onto a side street. He knew the area, had been there on assignment a few times.

He glanced in the rearview mirror. The van was a quarter mile back, still keeping its distance.

He stopped at a railroad crossing, watching in his review mirror as the van drove closer.

"What's going on?" Cassie asked, her voice raspy with sleep.

"Nothing." Yet.

"You're lying." She straightened in her seat, turning to look out the back window. "It's the van, isn't it?"

"I don't lie, and I don't know." Whether it was or not, didn't matter. What mattered was that it was obviously following them. He called the state police again and gave them an update on their location as he turned onto a rural road that led through a posh community of large homes.

In the distance, blue mountains pressed up against the cloud-laden sky. The first drop of rain fell as he exited the community, speeding onto a narrow two-lane highway. Farmland spread out to either side of it. No side roads. No place to hide if they had to find cover.

He glanced in the review mirror again. The van had accelerated, closing the distance between them. Gavin stepped on the gas, scanning the road ahead, looking for an opportunity to turn.

"He's getting closer," Cassie said, her body still twisted so that she could see out the back window.

"Tell you what, Cassie. How about you turn around? We get hit from behind while you're sitting like that and you could break your back."

"Right about now," she murmured, turning to do what he'd suggested, "a broken back seems to be the least of our worries."

She was right about that. The van was flying toward them.

Up ahead, several mailboxes sat listlessly on the side of the road. Dented and dirty, they probably hadn't been used in years.

But, where there were mailboxes, there were homes.

Where there were homes, there were driveways. He needed to find one, park the SUV, get Glory out. If he managed that, they had a chance.

Seconds later, he saw the opportunity he'd been waiting for. Nearly hidden by heavy brush, the driveway was barely visible. He didn't brake, didn't want the driver of the van to know that he was turning.

The SUV's tires squealed as he skidded into the turn, accelerated forward.

Cassie screamed, and Glory let out a quick sharp bark in response.

The van's driver missed the turn, but it wouldn't take long for him to backtrack.

Gavin called in his location again, praying that the state police were close.

The SUV bumped over a rutted gravel drive that spilled out into a circular parking area. An old house stood at the edge of it, the front door hanging from a hinge, the windows broken. A thick copse of trees crowded the edges of an overgrown yard.

He stopped the SUV and opened the door.

"What are you doing?" Cassie cried, her eyes wide and emerald green in the gloomy light.

"We stay in the SUV, and we're sitting ducks. We get out, and we've got a chance." He grabbed her hand, dragging her over the console and out of the vehicle.

Glory paced her kennel, whining softly. She sensed danger, knew it was coming for them. He opened the hatchback, snapped her lead on. She jumped out immediately, her gaze focused on the driveway and the road beyond it.

"Danger! Guard!" Gavin commanded.

Glory tensed, her scruff standing on end as she

growled low in her throat. Other than that soft warning, the day was silent. No roaring engine. No squeal of tires. Nothing.

That should have been comforting.

It wasn't.

"Come on," he whispered close to Cassie's ear.

For once, she didn't question him, just ran beside him as he rounded the house, making a beeline for the trees. They were out of sight of the road, out of range for a handgun, but Gavin's skin crawled, everything in him shouting that they were in the crosshairs of someone's firearm.

Glory growled again, swiveling on her lead and facing the way they'd come. He heeded the warning, tackling Cassie to the ground as the first bullet flew. It slammed into a tree an inch from his head, and he rolled onto his side, Glory crouched low as he took aim and fired.

Cassie jerked, mumbling something that he thought might have been a prayer.

There was no returning fire, and Gavin knew the gunman was probably moving into a better position, trying to get a kill-shot vantage point.

Wasn't going to happen.

Not on Gavin's watch.

He touched Cassie's cheek, then motioned toward the trees. "Stay low," he said.

She nodded her understanding, belly-crawling forward and into the thick copse of trees. Gavin unhooked Glory's lead, keeping his hand on her collar as he followed. He'd make sure Cassie was well hidden, and then he was going after the shooter.

Let him think he was the hunter.

In reality, he was going to be the prey.

THIRTEEN

They were being hunted.

Cassie could almost feel the eyes of the hunter, feel the hot breath of his pursuit as she slid through wet leaves, crawled over a fallen log and dropped onto the other side of it.

Rain poured down, soaking through her sweatshirt and her jeans as she army-crawled deeper into the trees.

Was Gavin behind her?

She couldn't hear him, couldn't hear much of anything over the slush of blood in her ears and the loud panting of her breath.

She needed to calm down. She wasn't going to do herself or Gavin any good if she went into full-out panic.

Something touched her ankle, and she jerked her leg away, just barely managing to bite back a scream.

She looked back, saw Gavin moving up behind her, Glory crouched low beside him. They were in sync, Glory's movements timed to match Gavin's.

Gavin reached her side and brushed strands of hair from her eyes. "You okay?" he mouthed, and she nodded, because she had no choice but to be fine. "They're on foot," he whispered, the sound barely carrying above the pounding rain.

"They?" she whispered.

"I'm assuming there's more than one and hoping that I'm wrong. Come on. I'm going to find a place for you to lie low. Then Glory and I are going to take them down."

He glanced around, motioned for her to follow as he crawled toward an upended oak. The root system had been exposed to the elements for years, the wood rotting and gnarled with weeds and dead leaves.

"This will work," he said, pulling back a handful of roots to reveal the cavernous hole beneath.

She climbed down, wet earth raining down on her head as she crouched beneath the root system.

Gavin leaned down, his lips brushing her ear as he spoke. "Stay in here until I come back for you."

"Maybe you should stay with me," she suggested, because if there was more than one shooter, more than one maniac searching for them, she didn't want Gavin to be outnumbered and overpowered. "Let the police handle the shooter."

"I am the police," he said with a gentle smile.

That smile—it did something to her. It made her think about all the things she used to dream of. It made her imagine that she could have them.

"I know, but. ."

"What?" He touched her cheek, his fingers warm against her chilled flesh.

"I don't want anything to happen to you."

"And, I don't want anything to happen to you. So stay here. Be quiet and don't even poke your head up until you see my face again." He let the roots fall over her hiding place, leaving her in darkness interspersed with hints of gray light. The root system provided enough cover

to keep her hidden, but she could see glimpses of leaves and trees, of rain splashing onto the ground.

She shivered, the cold seeping so deep into her bones that she didn't think she'd ever be warm again. She pulled her knees up to her chest, resting her chin on them.

She wasn't sure how much time had passed. A few minutes? More?

The woods were silent but for the rain padding on ground.

That scared her more than noise would have.

Footfall sounded somewhere close by, feet padding through mud and puddles. She tensed, watching as a shadow moved past her hiding place.

The gunman?

She thought it might be.

She could see boots, the cuffs of jeans.

What if he looked down and saw her through the roots system?

She wanted to scoot back, but she was afraid to move, afraid to breathe.

In the distance, sirens were blaring, the sound filtering through the trees and the ground. Help was on the way, but she wondered if it would be too late. If maybe she'd be dead before the police ever arrived.

Whoever was standing near her shelter moved. Slowly. Deliberately. As if he had all the time in the world. She followed his booted feet as he moved to the left of the root system. Stopped there.

Did he know she was hiding there?

Had he sensed her presence?

She needed a weapon. Just in case.

She slid her hand across the dirt floor, fingers gliding over leaves and earth as she searched for something

she could defend herself with. There were small rocks, dead leaves, a couple of miniscule twigs. Nothing that she thought could do much damage.

The sound of more footsteps made her freeze, and she looked up, surprised to see that the guy with the boots was standing in the same position. As she watched, a second set of ankles and feet appeared. No boots on this guy. He wore running shoes and dark jeans.

She could hear voices, but couldn't make out words. Whatever they were saying, the conversation was too muted for her to hear.

That was fine. If they were discussing the best way to drag her out from beneath the roots, she didn't want to know it.

Her fingers drifted over a larger rock, and she grasped it in her fist. Somehow the heavy weight of it was comforting. If she couldn't hit one of the gunmen with it, she could toss it as distraction.

Where was Gavin?

Somewhere close by?

And, Glory? Was she ready to attack?

She hoped so, praying the German shepherd could take both men down.

The police were getting closer, the sirens louder. Cassie's pulse jumped, and she caught her breath. Would the gunmen run? Or would they keep looking?

Please, let them run, she prayed silently.

A dog growled, the sound vicious and brutal.

And, then the world went wild. Snarling, howling dog. Cursing men. Rain pouring. Something blocked Cassie's view, speeding past the cracks in the root system so quickly Cassie could barely track the movement.

Glory?

One of the men shouted, his cry for help ringing in Cassie's ears. She wanted to look away, but she couldn't stop watching. Glory had one of the guys by the arm, was pulling him down to the ground.

The other guy moved in. Cassie could see just enough to know he was holding a knife.

"Glory," she yelled, and knew her mistake immediately.

The dog could take care of herself. She was trained to do it.

Cassie should have kept her mouth shut.

Too late. The root system was ripped back, leaves and debris falling into the hole. Hands reached in, a face she knew too well appearing. Just like in her nightmares, he had cold dead eyes and blond hair.

She screamed as he grabbed her arm and tried to haul her out of the pit. She went fighting and shouting for help, her frantic struggles doing nothing to stop him.

Glory snapped and growled, her focus on the second man. Cassie couldn't see his face; she caught only a glimpse of his dark hair as he tried to free his wrist from the dog's mouth.

Fingers curled around Cassie's neck and cold metal pressed to her temple. She thought she was going to die, that she was going to leave all the kids with Virginia, that Gavin was going to have to explain her death to them the same way Cassie had explained so many things.

"One down. One to go," the guy growled, his eyes as cold and hard as they'd been the night she'd first seen him. "Tell you what. You tell me which kid was at Jeffries's house, and I'll give you a running start."

She knocked the guy's hand away, stomped on his instep.

His grip loosened, and she yanked away, diving behind a tree that she hoped would provide cover. Something slammed into her upper arm seconds before she heard the gun report.

She didn't feel pain, didn't feel anything except the warm ooze of blood down her arm.

Someone shouted, but she didn't stop. She had to make it back to the kids, had to make it back to Virginia.

Another gunshot rang through the quiet copse of trees, and another. Either help had arrived or Gavin was shooting. Either way, she hoped the gunman was down. He'd done enough damage to Harland's family, to Cassie's. Maybe even to Rosa's.

She stumbled, her feet sticking to the wet earth as she tried to put more distance between herself and the gunfight. Men shouted. Feet pounded. A dog barked over and over again. All of it seemed muted, the gloomy light faded.

She stumbled again, fell to her knees, and realized that blood was dripping from her fingers onto the ground.

Get up, her brain screamed, but her body wasn't cooperating.

She swayed, telling herself that she wasn't going to pass out, that she wouldn't be lying on the ground unconscious when the gunman caught up with her.

If he caught up.

He could be dead.

"Cassie!"

She knew Gavin's voice, heard the panic in it.

She wanted to turn and tell him that she was okay, that everything was going to be fine, but darkness was edging in, the cool gray day turning to pitch-black night. She toppled over, her arms refusing to break her fall.

Someone's did. Hands wrapped around her waist, and she was lowered to the ground.

"Cassie!" Gavin growled. "Open your eyes."

"I'd rather not," she said, her words slurred, her brain moving sluggishly.

He laughed, the sound shaky and rough.

She forced her eyes open, looking into his face. "Don't worry, Gavin. I'm not planning to die on you."

"No?" He pulled his shirt off and pressed it against the wound in her arm.

The pain she hadn't been feeling was suddenly there, searing up her arm and across her shoulder.

"Of course not," she managed to say through gritted teeth.

"Good, because if you did, I wouldn't get a chance to say what I need to." He wiped rain from her face with his free hand, his touch tender and light.

"What's that?" she asked, because she wanted to know, needed to know.

"That I told you to stay hidden until you saw me," he muttered. "And that I hope that maybe one day you'll start to listen to me instead of going maverick all the time."

"That's it?" She laughed, the sound ending on a quiet groan.

Yeah. The pain was there and getting worse.

"No." He shook his head, his fingers skimming across her cheek and down to the pulse point in her neck. "I also want to tell you that if something had happened to you, I'd have spent the rest of my life wondering what I'd missed out on."

"Gavin—"

"You're not like other woman I've known, Cassie.

Your priorities are different, your focus is different. You're not thinking about a future with a husband and kids and a white picket fence, you're planning a lifetime with children who need you as much as you seem to need them."

"I do need them," she admitted. She felt woozy, lightheaded, her thoughts scattering to the winds as fast as they could form, but there was something *she* needed to say. "And, you," she admitted, and thought she saw him smile.

She wasn't sure, though, because her vision had faded, her thoughts gone, and she was carried on waves of pain into the darkness.

Cassie had nearly died.

The weight of that settled on his shoulders and stayed there as he paced the hospital waiting room. They'd taken her to surgery three hours ago. He hadn't heard anything since then. That worried him. The wound had been in the fleshy part of her upper arm, but it had bled a lot. Too much. He could still see it puddled on wet earth, seeping through slick leaves.

"Pacing isn't going to get her through surgery any sooner," Brooke commented, not even bothering to look up from the magazine she was rifling through. She and Adam Donovan sat a few feet away. Brooke had come to offer support. Adam had come to help with protection detail. Ace lay on the floor beside him, relaxed as he waited for the command to guard.

"Maybe it won't, but it's helping me keep my sanity," Gavin responded, grabbing a cup from a stack near a coffeemaker and pouring himself a cup of dark brew. It was lukewarm and bitter, but he drank it, anyway.

"You know it's not your fault that she was shot, right?" Adam commented.

"Then whose fault was it?" he bit out, because it felt like his fault.

"The guy who pulled the trigger. The fact that he paid the ultimate price doesn't change the fact that he was guilty."

True, and the fact that he'd been shot dead by a state trooper didn't get them any closer to finding Michael's killer. Harland had said the shooter was around five foot eight. The dead-eyed guy and his partner in crime were both taller than that.

"I wish we could have taken him and his partner in alive," Gavin muttered, taking another sip of the lukewarm coffee.

"They got what they deserved," Brooke responded. "We'll get an ID on both of them, figure out who their associates are." She shrugged. "It'll be more than we had yesterday."

"And less than I wanted." Gavin tossed the cup into a trash can.

"At least the guy who wanted Cassie dead is out of the picture."

"He wasn't Michael's murderer, though. Neither was his accomplice." The blue-eyed man had been five-eleven. His partner had been over six-foot.

"I know. I read the state police report. Neither man matched Harland's description," Brooke agreed.

"Find anything of use in that report?" Adam asked.

"Nothing worth mentioning." She stood and stretched. "The van they used was reported stolen this morning. The keys were in the ignition. No prints on them. Nothing useable on the van, either. They were careful."

"Makes me think it wasn't their first walk around the block," Adam responded.

"It also makes me think they're part of something bigger." Gavin walked to the waiting room doorway. Cassie should be out of surgery. "They were too good at what they did. Too confident, and they made sure to leave nothing behind. Neither had IDs. No prints in the van. They wore gloves the entire time."

"Professional hit men?" Brook suggested.

"That's what I was thinking," Gavin said. "I'm thinking that the guy Cassie saw at All Our Kids was hired to take out whichever child was at Harland's house."

"But Cassie saw him, and he had to get rid of her?" Brooke set the magazine down.

"Exactly."

"It's an interesting theory. Of course, the guy is dead, so we can't ask him to confirm it." Adam poured coffee, sipped it and frowned.

"The coroner will identify him eventually." Gavin was counting on that, praying for it. "When he does, I think we'll find that he had a sudden windfall of cash."

"What we need to find, is Erin Eagleton. I want to hear what she has to say. She was at Harland's place the night Michael was killed. I want to know what she saw."

"We all do." A person didn't disappear without a good reason. Gavin was anxious to find out what Erin's was. Had she seen something?

Or had she pulled the trigger and run from her crime?

"You think she was involved in the murder? MVA records have her as height as five-foot-seven. That's pretty close to the five-eight Harland described."

"I don't want to speculate. I want to bring her in for questioning."

"That would be a lot easier if she hadn't disappeared off the face of the earth," Adam said, taking another sip of coffee.

"I don't think she's gone quite that far," Gavin responded. She'd disappeared. That was for sure, but they'd find her. Eventually. And, they'd find Michael's killer.

He glanced out the waiting room door. He wanted to hear from the surgeons, wanted to know for sure that Cassie was going to be okay. He'd been assured she would be, that the gunshot had torn through flesh and muscle and nicked an artery, but that it would heal well once it was cleaned out and closed.

"A watched pot never boils," Adam said cryptically.

Gavin would have smiled, if he hadn't been so scared for Cassie.

"And a surgeon waited on never arrives?" he asked.

"Something like that. Now, sit down. You're making Ace nervous."

He was making himself nervous, so he dropped into a chair. If Glory had been with him, she'd have nudged his hand, whined for a little of his attention. He'd sent her back to the safe house with Isaac. After nearly losing Cassie, he wanted double guards and dogs on the house and the kids.

"I'm thinking Cassie isn't going to be up to that meeting with Rosa Gomez's sister tomorrow," Brooke said. "Should we reschedule?"

"I think Margaret is already on top of that," Adam replied. "She put in a call to Harland, and he's contacting CPS. They're going to try to arrange for Lana to come here."

"Good. Juan is a cute kid, and I think he'll do a lot better if his aunt knows the things he likes."

"Cassie will meet with Rosa's sister if she's up to it. If she's not, it's going to have to wait," Gavin responded. Right at that moment, he wasn't all that worried about the meeting with Rosa's sister. He wasn't worried about anything but finding out that Cassie was okay.

Footsteps sounded in the hall, and Gavin jumped up; he was halfway to the door when Cassie's surgeon appeared. Tall and thin with a long face and dark eyes, she wore green scrubs and a kind smile.

"Good news," she said. "Cassie is doing great. I was able to clean and close the wound, repair a couple of ligaments. She'll have limited use of that arm for a while, but in time, she'll be nearly back to normal."

"Can I see her?" Gavin asked, already in the hall and moving down it. He knew where surgery was, could guess where the recovery rooms were.

"Captain McCord," the surgeon said, and touched his arm. "You're welcome to see her, but you're going to have to wait to interview her. She's just coming out of the anesthesia. Nothing she says will be admissible in a court of law."

"I understand." And he didn't care. He wasn't planning an interview, had no intention of questioning Cassie about what she'd seen or heard. Not while she was lying in a hospital bed recovering from surgery.

There'd be time for that.

He'd make sure of it.

But, right now, all he wanted to do was see Cassie, make sure that she really was okay.

"Come this way, then." The surgeon headed down the long corridor, turned right and kept walking. Cassie's room was at the end of the hall, the door closed.

"She's going to need to take it easy for a couple of

days, but we'll probably only keep her for twenty-four hours. Is there someone who can help her at home? She won't be able to lift things, might need some help with daily activities. Physical therapy will start working with her once the stitches are out, but until then, she's going to have to be careful."

"There will be people to help," Gavin said, pushing open the door and walking into the quiet hospital room.

Cassie lay still, her hair pulled back with a black head-band, the silky red strands spread out on the pillow. She'd lost all color, her skin so pale it was almost translucent.

His heart lurched, guilt weighing him down.

He'd failed her.

He touched her hand, his fingers skimming across her knuckles. He thought she'd be unaware, but she turned her hand, wove her fingers through his.

"Gavin," she said without opening her eyes.

"Maybe," he replied, some of his worry easing as she smiled.

"For sure. I'd know you if I were blindfolded and standing in a dark room."

"Would you?" He ran his thumb across her wrist, felt her pulse fluttering beneath her skin.

"Yes. You smell like the outdoors, like fall, like cool evenings on the front porch."

If he'd been a blushing man, his cheeks would have gone a few shades of red. He wasn't, so he lifted her hand and pressed a kiss to her knuckles. "Thanks. I think."

"Oh, it's a compliment." She finally opened her eyes, her gaze hazy and a little unfocused. "I don't normally notice those kinds of things, but with you—"

"Cassie," he cut in. "You might want to wait to pour your heart out until after the anesthesia wears off."

"I had anesthesia?" She frowned and tried to sit up, her hospital gown sliding off her shoulder and revealing the thick bandages around her upper arm. "Why?"

"You were shot, remember?"

"Shot?" She looked at her bandaged arm. "Wow. Who knew?"

"Me and everyone who was there when it happened."

"The kids are going to love hearing about it. Once I can remember." Her eyes drifted closed, and he thought she'd fallen asleep.

He wanted to call Virginia, let her know that Cassie was out of surgery. The woman had been in hysterics when he'd called the first time. He'd had to dispatch extra officers to calm her down and help with the kids.

He tried to pull his hand from Cassie's but she held on tight, her grip firmer than he would have expected.

"Don't go, Gavin," she whispered.

"Are you afraid? Because the guy who was after you, he's dead. You're safe."

"He is? That's good and, maybe, a little sad. But I wasn't afraid." She opened her eyes, looked straight at him. No haziness now. No lack of focus. She was there, asking him for something he'd thought he could never give. "I just don't want to wake up alone. Promise me I won't."

He had things to do, phone calls to make, a case that needed solving. With Cassie, though, he couldn't deny the request.

"I promise," he said, and he meant it for that day and for tomorrow and for every day as long as Cassie needed him.

Maybe she knew that. Maybe she understood.

She squeezed his fingers, pulled his hand in and pressed a kiss to his knuckles.

He thought she was sealing his promise, thought that she was offering one of her own.

He didn't pull away when her hand dropped back to the bed, didn't move as the clock ticked by the minutes and then the hours.

His phone rang, but he didn't answer it, because right at that moment, he knew why men got married, why work became only part of their lives. He understood why passion for justice could be weighed by compassion for someone, and he knew that he was about to find balance in his life, space in it for something other than his work. Space in it for Cassie, for her crew of kids, for the home she loved and the job she did.

That made him smile.

Cassie shifted, turning her head, her eyes open again.

"I'm glad," she said, her words distinct, her eyes clear. "To see that you're a man of your word."

"Did you expect anything else?" he asked.

"I expected that I'd never find someone like you, but I guess it's happened. That being the case, I guess I'm going to have to get used to having one more person in my life."

"And a dog?" he asked, tucking the covers around her shoulders.

"A dog, too."

He laughed, and she smiled. "Now, you'd better go do your job, Gavin."

"I told you I'd stay."

"Until I woke up." She sat up, frowned. "And, I remember getting shot, so I guess I'm in my right mind. That means you are free to go."

"I'd rather stay."

"I'd rather know that you're out there protecting the world, Gavin, and that when you're done, you'll be back protecting me." She said it quietly, said it with so much sincerity, he knew it was true.

"Count on it," he responded, pressing a gentle kiss to her lips.

"Wow!" she breathed. "Destiny is going to die when I tell her about this."

"Do you plan to?"

"Years from now. Maybe right before you walk her down the aisle."

He liked the idea of that. He liked it a lot.

So, he kissed Cassie again.

To give her a little more to tell Destiny.

Then he said goodbye and headed out into the hall, leaving Cassie so that he could go to work, and so that he could return to her.

FOURTEEN

He chased her through the woods, sprinting after Cassie with so much speed, so much energy, she knew she'd never outrun him. Up ahead, an old house stood stark and lonely against the steel-gray sky. She ran toward it, footsteps pounding behind her.

Almost there!

She reached the rickety porch steps, tried to run up them, but the steps were quicksand, and all she could do was fall forward, catch herself with her arm.

Pain shot through her, and she screamed. Or tried to. Nothing emerged but a quiet moan.

And he was still coming.

She didn't want to look back, didn't want to see him bounding toward her, his eyes dead, his expression blank. She didn't want to see the gun or the knife or whatever it was that he planned to use to finish what he'd started.

She grabbed the stair railing, tried to pull herself up, but her fingers refused to grip the old wood, and she moaned again, tried again.

"Cassie!" the man whispered, his voice sending shivers up her spine.

She had to get up. Had to keep going.

"Cassie," he said again, his hand on her cheek.

She screamed, jerked upright so fast, she nearly smacked into the man who was standing over her.

Not the icy-eyed killer who'd died.

Harland.

In her bedroom.

She glanced around. Realized she wasn't at All Our Kids. Wasn't at the safe house. She was in a hospital room, the television muted, the bluish light from the screen flickering.

"Everyone okay in here?" A uniformed police officer walked in, his gaze jumping from Harland to Cassie. "Are you okay, ma'am?"

"I'm in the hospital." She glanced at her arm, at the IV line that snaked out of it. She remembered waking up, remembered Gavin being with her. Remembered a kiss, a conversation, remembered him leaving. She'd fallen asleep after that. She didn't know how long she'd been out, but it must have been a while. "With an IV line stuck in my arm. I don't think that counts as okay."

Someone chuckled.

Not someone.

Gavin. She'd know his laughter anywhere. Recognize his voice, his scent, his smile. She turned her head, saw him sitting in a chair, a laptop on a small table in front of him.

"You're back."

"I just had to file a report. I checked on the kids while I was at it. They're all fine."

"Is Virginia?"

He hesitated. "She will be. Once the sedative wears off."

"They had to sedate her?" Poor Virginia. She really

did need to learn how to handle emergencies and drama better.

"It was a mild sedative," Gavin responded. As if that made it better.

"Enough about Virginia. How are you, my dear?" Harland asked, his face haggard, his eyes deeply shadowed. "That's what we're all wondering."

"I'm alive, so I'd say I'm excellent. And, that I'm ready to go home." She sat up and swung her legs over the side of the bed.

"You really don't think you're going to get up, do you?" Gavin asked.

"Do you really think I'm not? I've got eight kids waiting for me. I can't be lying around in a hospital bed."

"You were shot," Harland said. "I think that is more than reason to be away from the kids."

"To you, maybe, but not to the kids. Where are my clothes?"

"Soaked with blood," Gavin responded.

"I guess I'll have to go in this." She plucked at the cotton hospital gown.

"Cassie." Harland put a hand on her arm. "Be reasonable."

"I am being reasonable. The kids have been through a lot. The last thing they need is to have me suddenly disappear."

"You didn't disappear. You needed medical treatment. Every one of those kids can understand that." Harland ran a hand over his hair, shook his head. "I had no idea you were this stubborn when I hired you."

"Sure you did. You liked my spunk, remember? You thought that my determination would give me an upper hand with the kids."

"And now you're throwing my words back in my face." He glanced at his watch, frowned. "Margaret and I arranged to have Rose's sister come here to speak with you. I know you're as anxious to make Juan's transition smooth as everyone else. You really should stay so that the two of you can talk."

"I'll stick around to talk to her, but I'm not going to stay the night."

"You're being unreasonable." He scowled.

"I'm being a mother. Isn't that what you hired me to do? And a mother's heart is always for her kids. They need me. Now more than ever." She stood on shaky legs and tried to tell her body that she was as fine as she wanted to be. Too bad her head was swimming. Too bad she felt a little sick. She wanted to march out the door, march down the hall, get in Gavin's SUV and return to the kids, but she wasn't sure she could take one step, let alone a few hundred.

"Right. Okay. You do what you think is best, but don't expect me to be happy about it. I'm going to see if Lana has arrived yet." He walked out of the room, muttering something about stubborn females as he went.

"He's not happy," Gavin pointed out.

"That's pretty obvious." She took a step, thought she might be able to take another. She didn't know where she was going. Gavin was her ride back to the kids, and he was leaning against the wall, arms crossed over his chest.

"I'm not happy, either."

"But you're going to take me to the safe house, anyway, right?"

"If I don't, will I still get to walk Destiny down the aisle one day?"

She blushed, remembering her words, his kiss, the

way she'd felt when she'd woken and seen him beside her bed. "I was under the influence when I said that."

"So you didn't mean it?"

"I—" She couldn't lie. Not to Gavin. Not ever. "I did. And, you can still walk her down the aisle. If she ever gets married. She might not. The girl is very prickly."

"We'll work on that. After I get you back to the safe house."

"You're going to take me?"

"Cassie, I couldn't deny you anything." He pushed the call button to summon the nurse.

Ten minutes later, she was in a wheelchair being pushed through the corridor, Gavin to her left, Adam to her right, all of them heading to a small meeting room where Lana and Harland were waiting. Cassie had told Gavin she was up to the meeting, but she wasn't so sure she was. She felt a little dizzy and a little sick, but she wanted to see the woman who was going to be Juan's mother. She wanted to tell her that he liked Cheerios and animal crackers and that he loved being sung to while he fell asleep.

She'd only had Juan for a few days, but she felt as though she'd known him his entire life. Thinking about saying goodbye to the little boy made her throat hot and her eyes burn. She wouldn't cry. She never cried when one of her foster kids left. She wanted them to know she was happy for them, that she believed that wherever they were going was going to be the best place for them.

She rubbed at a smudge of dirt on her thigh, refused to let herself think about goodbyes. She'd rather think about hellos and how wonderful it would be for Lana to meet her nephew.

"You doing okay?" Gavin asked, his fingers brushing her arm.

"Sure," she managed to say past the tightness in her throat.

She'd managed to pull on her dirty jeans, but her shirt hadn't been salvageable. Gavin had wrapped his jacket around her shoulder, pulling it into place over the hospital gown. She snuggled into it, refusing to glance in his direction. She didn't want him to see moisture in her eyes and think she was actually crying.

They reached the end of the corridor, and Adam opened the door. Gavin thanked the nurse and pushed the wheelchair into the room. Harland was there, standing beside a young woman who had the same dark hair and eyes as Rose.

"You must be Lana," Cassie said, offering her hand.

"And you're Cassie. Thank you for taking care of my nephew while the police were looking for me."

"It was my pleasure. He's a very sweet boy. I know you're going to love him. I only wish that…"

"My sister hadn't had to die for me to meet Juan?" Lana asked.

"Yes."

"I feel the same." She walked to a chair, took a seat, pulled a small pad of paper and a pen from her purse. "The congressman said that you could tell me about Juan. What he likes to eat. What time he goes to bed."

"I'd be happy to." She filled Lana in on every detail she could think of, watching as the other woman scribbled notes. Lana cared. It was obvious she wanted Juan to feel comfortable and happy.

And that made Cassie happy.

When she finished speaking, Lana stood. "Thank you.

This is going to be very helpful. I'm not sure I'll see you again. I'll be contacting a lawyer to start the process of petitioning for custody. If I have any questions, will it be possible to reach you?"

"Of course. I'm—"

"Harland can contact her for you, or you can contact CPS," Gavin cut in.

"Great," Lana said, hurrying to the door. "Thanks, again. I'd better go."

"I'll walk you out," Harland said. "You go get some rest, Cassie." He threw the words over his shoulder as he walked into the corridor with Lana.

"What did you think?" Adam asked as soon as Harland and Lana left the room.

"About?" Gavin asked as he pushed Cassie's wheelchair out of the room. They could wait for the nurse to come back, but he didn't want to. The sooner he got Cassie back to the safe house, the better he'd feel.

"The sister."

"Seems like she's going to take good care of her nephew. Why do you ask?"

"She seemed a little anxious to me."

"I'd be anxious if I were going to take custody of a two-year-old I've never met," Cassie said quietly. "Especially if that child was grieving the loss of his mother."

"I guess you've got a point," Adam responded, punching the button of the elevator. "We going out the service door?"

"My SUV is parked in the service lot. I figure the more careful we are, the less likely it is anyone will find the safe house."

"And the mitten-dropping kid? Wish whoever it was

would open his mouth and admit it," Adam said as they walked onto the elevator. "If he saw the killer, if we can get a description, that'll make our job easier."

"Our job is going to be difficult any way you cut it, Adam," Gavin responded. They had to find out who'd dropped the mitten, had to find Erin. Either of those things could break the case wide-open. Neither was going to be easy.

Cassie didn't say a word.

Her eyes were glassy, her face pale. She probably needed to go back to her hospital bed. She wanted to go home, though.

Or, at least, back to where her kids were.

He wasn't sure how much rest she'd get there, but she probably would be safer. Much as he'd like her to stay in the hospital, he had to admit, having her at the safe house was going to make protecting her easier.

She remained silent as he pushed her out of the service door and into cool March air. His SUV was a few feet away, parked close to the building. Adam went first, Ace loping along beside him. If there'd been any danger, he'd have alerted.

They were safe.

For now.

He pushed Cassie to the SUV, was leaning over to lift her from the chair when she opened her eyes. "I think I can manage," she said.

"Sure you can. But why should you?" He didn't give her a chance to respond, just lifted her and set her into the passenger seat.

"You want me to follow you back?" Adam asked.

"It's probably a good idea."

Gavin got in the SUV, turned on the engine, waited

until Adam pulled up behind him, the drove out of the parking lot.

Cassie had closed her eyes. She opened them as they started moving. "Do you think we'll be followed?" she asked.

"Not by anyone but Adam."

"Are you sure? Because if I'm going to be shot again, I'd like to be prepared for it."

"I'm not sure that's something you can prepare for," he said, glancing in the review mirror. No one behind him but Adam. That was exactly how he wanted things.

"I'd at least like to try."

"How about you try to rest instead? We've got a long drive ahead of us, and you need to rest."

"I rested in the hospital."

"You should have stayed longer. You're going home to a house filled with kids."

"And a hysterical assistant," she added. "Trust me. I know. But they're family, and I miss them."

"They miss you, too. Destiny asked to come to the hospital with me. She's angry that I wouldn't let her."

"Did you tell her she was in danger?"

"I tried. She wouldn't listen to reason." The teen had argued for twenty minutes, and she'd still been arguing when Gavin walked out the door.

She'd tried to run after his SUV, and Brooke had had to force her back into the house.

Gavin felt bad about it. Worse than he'd expected to. The kid was growing on him. Which was good, because he planned to be a part of her life for as long as she was part of Cassie's.

"I'll talk to her when we get home."

Home?

It was a safe house, but he had to admit, it felt more like home than his apartment did. Felt more like it than anyplace he'd ever been. Even All Our Kids had never been home. Not while he'd been there. It had been a place to stay, a place where he was cared for and cared about. Home, though. That was something different. That was something that happened when a place was filled with family.

By the time he made it back to the safe house, the sun was going down, the sky pink with fading daylight. Cassie slept soundly, her head against the window, her wounded arm held in her lap.

She shifted as he parked the SUV, groaning as he turned off the ignition.

"Cassie?" He touched her cheek, and she opened her eyes, looked into his face.

"Are we home?" she asked as the safe house door flew open, and kids came streaming out.

His heart jumped as he saw them—the abandoned, the neglected, the abused.

The *loved*, because Cassie had come into their lives.

The *accepted*, because she cared for them just the way they were.

"Yes," he said, and she glanced out the window, saw the kids, smiled the kind of smile that showed true joy and love and happiness.

He leaned in to taste it on her lips, to feel the joy that curved her mouth.

"Wow!" she said as he pulled away. "Wait until I tell Virginia about this."

"On her wedding day?"

"No." She laughed, opening her door and preparing to greet her family. "As soon as that sedative wears off.

Because I've got to tell you, Gavin, a kiss like that isn't something a woman can keep to herself."

He would have responded, but the kids were there, shouting and shrieking and filling Cassie in on everything she'd missed.

He watched as Destiny helped her out of the car, putting an arm around her waist.

The teen met his eyes, scowled, her eyes filled with worry and with relief.

"Well…don't just sit there smiling like a fool," she barked. "Come on around and help me."

She had a mouth on her, that kid.

He'd have to work on that.

First, though, he'd do what she asked.

FIFTEEN

She'd been kissed.

Thoroughly.

By a guy who'd saved her life so many times she'd lost count.

Cassie had spent the past week smiling about it.

Which had annoyed Destiny, but Cassie didn't care.

Happiness was a gift that should be shared.

Unfortunately, she hadn't had a lot of time to share it with Gavin. He'd been working hard, chasing down leads, trying to identify a suspect. The guy who'd tried to burn down All Our Kids had been identified, his bank account accessed. He'd deposited ten thousand dollars cash in it the day after Michael's murder. There'd been no way to track the cash. No way of knowing who it had come from.

Gavin wasn't happy about that.

Cassie knew that for sure.

What she didn't know was how long she and the kids were going to be trapped in the safe house. It wasn't that it was bad; it was just that it wasn't home. No matter how hard she tried to make it that.

She rubbed the back of her neck, wincing as muscles in her shoulder pulled. Her arm hurt.

Her head ached.

She felt like she'd been run over by a truck. Twice.

But, Cassie was alive, and she'd be forever grateful for that. Even if the kids *were* driving her crazy.

"I have an idea," she said to no one in particular.

Only Rachel glanced her way. The rest of the kids were too busy bickering about who was on the schedule for kitchen cleanup.

"I said," she repeated with a lot more energy. "I have an idea."

That finally got a few heads to turn. "How about instead of arguing over who is supposed to do the dishes, you all pitch in and work together."

"That's a sweet idea," Destiny said, every bit of her preteen sarcasm coming out. "But, I did the dishes last night and the night before. It's Tommy's turn."

"It's not," Tommy shrieked. He'd been worse since Cassie was shot, spending more time in his room than out of it, hiding under the bed at night. Cassie had an appointment with his therapist, but getting to it was a problem. Aside from a trip to the doctor to have her wound checked she hadn't been out of the safe house in a week.

The kids were getting antsy.

She was getting antsy.

"Tommy," she said, trying her best to be patient. "Get the chore chart. If your name is on it—"

"I'm not getting any stupid chore chart!" he yelled, running from the kitchen, his footsteps pounding on the stairs. A door slammed, and she knew he'd locked himself into his room.

"I'd better go deal with that, Virginia. Would you mind taking the other kids outside for a while? I think being cooped up is getting to all of us."

"I'll do the dishes," Rachel volunteered with a fake cheerfulness that was another punch to Cassie's solar plexus. Ever since Cassie had been shot, Rachel had been doing everything in her power to be helpful. She'd cleaned her room, Cassie's room, the bathrooms. She'd made an attempt at making breakfast almost every morning and lunch almost every afternoon. She'd even admitted that she'd been down in the living room the night Michael was shot, that she'd put the television on mute and watched one of her favorite cartoons on the DVD. She'd heard footsteps on the stairs, turned off the television, watched as one of the boys walked through the foyer. She insisted that she didn't know which one it was, and Cassie believed her.

It was a shame that she hadn't seen more, and even more of a shame that she felt guilty about Cassie's injury. The poor kid was going to work herself sick trying to make up for something that wasn't her fault.

"That's okay, Rachel," Virginia said. "It's Tommy's turn, and he's going to have to do them. Just leave what's in the sink in the sink and get your shoes."

Cassie trudged up the stairs while Virginia organized an outdoor excursion. She'd had little energy since the shooting, but she was doing everything in her power to fake it. Virginia needed her to be strong. The kids needed her to be strong. She had no other choice but to do it. No matter how worn down she was.

She wiggled Tommy's doorknob. Locked. Just like she'd expected. "Tommy? Open the door?"

He didn't respond, and she stood on her tiptoes, trying to reach the key that lay on top of the doorjamb.

"What are you doing?" someone asked, and she

screamed, nearly falling over backward as she whirled to face Gavin.

"Where did you come from?" she gasped, her hand on her chest as if that could stop her heart's wild thumping.

"Outside."

"Smart aleck," she replied, and he smiled, his eyes going soft and tender, his lips so kissable she had to look away.

"I just finished meeting with the team. I'm off duty until Sunday afternoon."

"Really?" That explained his dark jeans and the gray T-shirt that clung to his chest like a second skin. He wore a shoulder holster, his gun strapped inside of it. No matter where he went, that was with him. So was Glory. She padded up beside Cassie, nosing the space at the bottom of the door.

"Really," he responded. "And now that I've answered your question maybe you can answer mine—what are you doing?"

"Trying to get Tommy out of his room."

"Again? What is this? The fourth time in a week?"

"Something like that."

"I'll get the key." He reached over her head, his chest pressed against her back, his arm sliding across her hair as he grabbed the key. "You're not supposed to be reaching above your head."

Was she supposed to lean into him, let herself rest against his strength? Because that's what she wanted to do.

"The doctor said I'm healing well and can go back to my normal routine."

"Did you forget that I was there? Or were you just

hoping that I'd forget that he also said you should take things slowly?"

"I am taking things slowly. I'm taking them so slowly that I'm driving myself batty. If I don't get out of this place for a while, I'll probably go stark raving mad!" She opened the door and stepped into the boys' room. Everything was neat and tidy, the room organized for maximum floor space. Only Tommy's bed was a mess, the stuffed animals piled in the center of it and spilling over onto the floor. She could see the top of Tommy's head nearly hidden by animals, could just make out a little hand clutching a bear.

"Are you hiding, Tommy?" Gavin asked, striding to the pile of animals and lifting one. Tommy burrowed deeper under his hoard, refusing to look at Gavin or Cassie.

"This isn't about cleaning the dishes, is it?" Cassie sat beside the pile of animals, and Gavin dropped down beside her.

There wasn't really enough room for two, but she didn't mind having him so close. His arm slid around her waist, and she didn't move away. She liked him like this—dressed in casual clothes, his hair a little ruffled, his jaw shadowed with the beginning of a beard. She liked the way it felt to be near him.

"It *is* about dishes," Tommy insisted, poking his head out from under the animals. "I don't want to do them."

"I wish that mattered, buddy," Cassie said. "But it doesn't. We don't always get to pick and choose what we want to do. Most of the time, we have to do a few things that we're not so fond of."

"Like school?" he muttered, sliding out from the massive pile and kneeling beside her. He was a cute kid,

a smart one. If he hadn't been mistreated, abused, neglected, he'd probably be an A student with all kinds of opportunities available to him.

"Exactly like school."

"I don't like school or dishes, and I don't want to do either!" Since he'd already completed his school assignments for the day, Cassie ignored the comment.

"Do you like flag football?" Gavin asked. "Because I picked up everything we need to play a game."

"You did?" Tommy frowned. "When? Because I didn't see no flag football stuff."

"This morning. When I went to meet with Juan's aunt. Of course, there's no way the game can be played if there are dishes in the sink."

"Why not?" Tommy asked, lifting a couple of stuffed animals and tossing them onto the pile.

"It's just a rule."

"I don't—"

"Tommy," Cassie broke in. "You either want to play flag football or you don't. If you do, the dishes have to be done."

He scowled, and she was sure he'd refuse. He'd been just that ornery lately. Apparently, flag football was too tempting to resist. He jumped off the bed. "Fine. I'll wash the stupid dishes!"

He raced down the hall, his feet pounding on the stairs.

"So how'd I do?" Gavin asked, pulling her to her feet.

"Bribery with flag football? It's a win," she replied, looking into his handsome face, his clear blue eyes. "Except that he still hasn't admitted to anything. He refuses to say he was outside the night of Michael's death."

"He'll get there. It's just going to take a little more

time." He tugged her closer, his hands on her waist, his fingers warm through her T-shirt.

"Since when did you become a paragon of patience?" she teased.

"Since I decided I might not end up a lifelong bachelor."

At his words, she stilled, her heart beating so hard, she thought it might burst from her chest. "I hadn't realized you'd planned to stay single."

"And I hadn't realized that there was a woman like you out in the world. If I had, I can guarantee you, it wouldn't have taken so long for us to meet."

"We met years ago."

"I guess you're right," he conceded. "We met each other, but we didn't really notice who it was we were looking at." His gaze drifted from her eyes, to her lips. "If we had, would we have missed out on this?" His lips brushed hers, and a thrill of excitement shot straight into her heart.

Not just for that moment, for that sweet, sweet kiss, but for Gavin, for his honesty and strength, for all the things that made him who he was.

"No," she whispered, breathless with joy, with contentment. "I don't suppose we would have."

He smiled and took her hand. "Once Michael's killer is caught, we're going to do something fun together. Something that doesn't involve separating kids, bribing little boys, cleaning up messes."

"Dodging bullets?"

"That, either."

"Do you think it will ever be over? It seems to me, you and your team have a lot of leads, but no solid evidence."

"It will end. We'll find Michael's killer."

"And Rosa's?"

"Yes. Hers, too." He led the way downstairs. Tommy was already at the sink, scrubbing dishes, water and bubbles splashing onto the floor.

"I hope you're right, Gavin. Rosa and Michael deserve justice. And the kids need to be home. They need to go to school, see their friends. Do all the things that normal kids do."

"They're going to be fine. As far as I can tell, they're having the time of their lives here."

"They act that way, but—"

"I thought we agreed that worry was a waste of energy. Seeing as how you believe that God is in control."

"My mouth agreed. My heart is a little more reluctant."

"It will be okay," he said, opening the back door and stepping outside. "Come on. You need a little fresh air."

"Where are we going?"

"Somewhere quiet," he responded, leading her across the grassy yard to an apple tree that was just beginning to bloom. He'd spread a blanket out underneath it and held it down with several small rocks. A picnic basket sat to one side of the blanket. Glory dropped down beside it, her tongue lolling out, her expression so rapturous, Cassie smiled.

"You've been busy, Gavin."

"I finally have some time on my hands," he responded. "I want to make the most of it."

"By having a picnic with your lead witness?"

"You're not a witness anymore. The guy you saw is dead," he reminded her.

"But the person who hired him isn't."

"Let's forget about that for a while, okay?" He touched her cheek and smiled.

And, she couldn't resist that smile or him.

"Okay."

"Because, I've been thinking about this picnic for a while. I've got it all planned out."

"Yeah?" she asked, dropping down onto the blanket.

"I brought enough food for an army." He glanced at the house. "Because I figured we were going to have to share."

"Do you mind?" she asked as the first kid walked around the side of the house, spotted them on the blanket and ran back. Probably to get the rest of the crew.

"Not a bit." He smiled and lay on his back so he was staring up at the boughs of the apple tree. "Did I ever tell you about Helena?" he asked.

"You know you didn't."

"And I know I want to. She and I were engaged a few years back. I thought she was everything I wanted, everything God wanted for me."

"What happened?" she asked, stroking his hair back from his forehead, enjoying the silky feel of it beneath her fingers.

"My job happened. She got tired of waiting for me. She got tired of dining alone. She got tired of playing second fiddle to my career. She broke things off in the parking lot of my apartment about a month before the wedding."

"I'm sorry," she said, and she meant it, because Gavin deserved better.

"I'm not. Helena was a great lady, but she had a problem. Something it took me a long time to recognize."

"Selfishness?"

"No." He chuckled. "The problem with Helena was that she wasn't you."

"I think that's the sweetest thing anyone has ever said to me," she responded, lying down beside him, a few inches separating their bodies. She could feel his presence, anyway, feel the warmth of his arm, his hip, his thigh.

Above her, thick old apple boughs twined together, their tiny green buds adding color to the gray-brown bark. Soon the tree would bloom, flowers would replace the buds. Eventually there'd be lush sweet apples.

Nothing could be as sweet as this moment, though.

Nothing could be quite as nice as lying beside Gavin, not touching, not speaking, just being together.

His fingers traced the curve of her arm, finding their way to her palm. He held her hand for the longest time as the sun drifted across the sky and kids' voices drifted on the air.

"I held them off as long as I could," Virginia hollered. "But, brace yourselves. They're on the way."

"I guess that's our cue," Gavin said.

"I guess it is. Thank you for the best picnic I've ever had."

"You didn't eat a thing," he said as he helped her to her feet.

"I did something better," she responded. "I spent time with you."

He smiled again, tugging her away from the tree, the blanket, the basket as the kids ran toward them, Virginia trudging along behind.

They had a long way to go, Cassie's little family. They had a lot more that they'd have to face, but she wasn't worried. Not anymore. She had Gavin, she had her faith

and she had all the time in the world to enjoy the life God had given her.

A good life, she thought as she looked at the kids.

A great one, her heart replied as Gavin squeezed her hand and led her back across the yard.

* * * * *

If you liked this CAPITOL K-9 UNIT *novel,*
watch for the next book in the series,
DUTY BOUND GUARDIAN by Terri Reed.

And don't miss a single story in the
CAPITOL K-9 UNIT *miniseries:*

Book #1: PROTECTION DETAIL
by Shirlee McCoy
Book #2: DUTY BOUND GUARDIAN
by Terri Reed
Book #3: TRAIL OF EVIDENCE
by Lynette Eason
Book #4: SECURITY BREACH
by Margaret Daley
Book #5: DETECTING DANGER
by Valerie Hansen
Book #6: PROOF OF INNOCENCE
by Lenora Worth

Dear Reader,

I was so excited when I was asked to take part in the 2015 Love Inspired Suspense continuity. When I found out that it was another K-9 continuity and that my heroine was a foster mother, I was over the moon! My husband and I adopted our youngest daughter five years ago. An orphan nearly from birth, she had been deemed unadoptable and lived in an orphanage in China for three years before her foster mother found her sitting in a hallway there. Liz was immediately taken with my blonde-haired blue-eyed daughter and begged to be allowed to foster her. Three months later, she was finally able to bring her home. Because of Liz's love, my daughter blossomed. She learned to walk, to talk, to feed herself. Most importantly, she learned to love. When we finally met her, she was a beautiful seven-year-old girl with all the spunk and personality that a child that age should have. Foster parenting is difficult work. It takes a special kind of person to do it and do it well. Writing *Protection Detail* allowed me to explore that. I hope you enjoy reading about Cassie and her crew of foster kids. Gavin is the perfect hero for the group. A former foster child, he is ready to put his life on the line to protect those he cares about. With his protection dog, Glory, at his side, he'll do whatever it takes to keep Cassie and her kids safe. I hope you enjoy the first in the Capitol K-9 Series. I love to hear from readers. If you have time, drop me a line at shirlee@shirleemccoy.com.

Shirlee McCoy

COMING NEXT MONTH FROM
Love Inspired® Suspense

Available April 7, 2015

DUTY BOUND GUARDIAN
Capitol K-9 Unit • by Terri Reed

A stolen art relic leads K-9 officer Adam Donovan to Lana Gomez as the prime suspect. Yet when the true thief tries to kill Lana, Adam must safeguard the gorgeous museum curator.

SECRET REFUGE
Wings of Danger • by Dana Mentink

The man who killed Keeley Stevens's sister is now threatening Keeley. Former parole officer Mick Hudson knows it's up to him to keep her out of harm's way and bring the criminal to justice.

TARGETED • by Becky Avella

Despite his recent injury, officer Rick Powell is determined to keep schoolteacher Stephanie O'Brien from becoming a serial killer's next victim.

ROYAL RESCUE • by Tammy Johnson

Ever since her father's murder, princess Thea James has lived in fear. Royal bodyguard Ronin Parrish promises he'll shield her from the attacker, but does he have ulterior motives?

PRESUMED GUILTY • by Dana R. Lynn

Framed for a crime she did not commit, Melanie Swanson must now trust a handsome policeman to protect her from becoming the real criminal's next target.

FATAL FREEZE • by Michelle Karl

Trapped aboard an icebound ferry with a dangerous crime ring, private investigator Lexie Reilly and undercover CIA agent Shaun Lane will need to work together if they want to survive.

LISCNM0315

REQUEST YOUR FREE BOOKS!
2 FREE RIVETING INSPIRATIONAL NOVELS
PLUS 2 FREE MYSTERY GIFTS

Love Inspired.
SUSPENSE

YES! Please send me 2 FREE Love Inspired® Suspense novels and my 2 FREE mystery gifts (gifts are worth about $10). After receiving them, if I don't wish to receive any more books, I can return the shipping statement marked "cancel." If I don't cancel, I will receive 4 brand-new novels every month and be billed just $4.74 per book in the U.S. or $5.24 per book in Canada. That's a savings of at least 21% off the cover price. It's quite a bargain! Shipping and handling is just 50¢ per book in the U.S. and 75¢ per book in Canada.* I understand that accepting the 2 free books and gifts places me under no obligation to buy anything. I can always return a shipment and cancel at any time. Even if I never buy another book, the two free books and gifts are mine to keep forever.

123/323 IDN F5AC

Name	(PLEASE PRINT)	
Address		Apt. #
City	State/Prov.	Zip/Postal Code

Signature (if under 18, a parent or guardian must sign)

Mail to the **Harlequin®** Reader Service:
IN U.S.A.: P.O. Box 1867, Buffalo, NY 14240-1867
IN CANADA: P.O. Box 609, Fort Erie, Ontario L2A 5X3

**Are you a current subscriber to Love Inspired Suspense books
and want to receive the larger-print edition?
Call 1-800-873-8635 or visit www.ReaderService.com.**

* Terms and prices subject to change without notice. Prices do not include applicable taxes. Sales tax applicable in N.Y. Canadian residents will be charged applicable taxes. Offer not valid in Quebec. This offer is limited to one order per household. Not valid for current subscribers to Love Inspired Suspense books. All orders subject to credit approval. Credit or debit balances in a customer's account(s) may be offset by any other outstanding balance owed by or to the customer. Please allow 4 to 6 weeks for delivery. Offer available while quantities last.

Your Privacy—The Harlequin® Reader Service is committed to protecting your privacy. Our Privacy Policy is available online at www.ReaderService.com or upon request from the Harlequin Reader Service.
We make a portion of our mailing list available to reputable third parties that offer products we believe may interest you. If you prefer that we not exchange your name with third parties, or if you wish to clarify or modify your communication preferences, please visit us at www.ReaderService.com/consumerschoice or write to us at Harlequin Reader Service Preference Service, P.O. Box 9062, Buffalo, NY 14269. Include your complete name and address.

LIS13R

SPECIAL EXCERPT FROM

Love Inspired
SUSPENSE

*Framed for a crime she didn't commit,
museum curator Lana Gomez must prove her
innocence under the watchful eyes of
Capitol K-9 Unit officer Adam Donovan.*

*Read on for a sneak preview of
the next exciting installment of the*
***CAPITOL K-9 UNIT** series,*
DUTY BOUND GUARDIAN
by *Terri Reed*.

K-9 officer Adam Donovan's cell buzzed inside the breast pocket of his uniform shirt. He halted, staying out of the rain beneath the overhang covering the entrance to the E. Barrett Prettyman Federal Courthouse.

"Sit," he murmured to his partner, Ace, a four-year-old, dark-coated, sleek Doberman pinscher. The dog obediently sat on his right. Keeping Ace's lead in his left hand, he answered the call. "Adam Donovan."

By habit Adam scanned the crowds of tourists flooding the National Mall, on alert for any criminal activity. Not even nighttime or an April drizzle could keep sight seers in their hotels. To his right the central dome of the US Capitol building gleamed with floodlights, postcard perfect.

"Gavin here" came the deep voice of his boss, Captain Gavin McCord. "You still at the courthouse?"

Adam had had a late meeting with the DA regarding a case against a drug dealer who'd been selling in and around the metro DC area. The elite Capitol K-9 Unit had been called in to assist the local police during a two-hour manhunt nine months ago. The K-9 unit was often enlisted in various crimes throughout the Washington, DC, area.

Ace had been the one to find the suspect hiding in a construction Dumpster outside of the National Gallery of Art. The suspect took the DA's deal and gave up the names of his associates rather than stand trial, which had been scheduled to begin later this week.

A victory on this rainy spring evening.

"Yes, sir."

"There's been a break-in at the American Museum and two of the museum employees have been assaulted," Gavin stated.

"Injured or dead?" Adam asked, already moving down the steps toward his vehicle with Ace at his heels.

"Injured. The intruder rendered both employees unconscious, but the security guard came to and pulled the fire alarm, scaring off the intruder. Both have been rushed to the hospital on Varnum Street." Gavin's tone intensified. "But the other victim is who I'm interested in. Lana Gomez."

Don't miss
DUTY BOUND GUARDIAN by Terri Reed,
available April 2015 wherever
Love Inspired® Suspense books and ebooks are sold.

www.Harlequin.com

Hannah edged closer to her. "I don't like storms."

Mary slipped an arm around her daughter. "Don't
worry. We'll be at Katie's house before the rain catches
us."

It turned out she was wrong. Big raindrops began hit-
ting her windshield. A strong gust of wind shook the
buggy and blew dust across the road. The sky grew
darker by the minute. She urged Tilly to a faster pace. She
should have stayed home.

A red car flew past her with the driver laying on the
horn. Tilly shied and nearly dragged the buggy into the
fence along the side of the road. Mary managed to right
her. "Foolish *Englischers*. We are over as far as we can
get."

The rumble of thunder became a steady roar behind
them. Tilly broke into a run. Hannah began screaming.
Mary glanced back and her heart stopped. A tornado had
dropped from the clouds and was bearing down on them.
Dust and debris flew out from the wide base.

Dear God, help me save my baby. What do I do?

She saw an intersection up ahead.

Bracing her legs against the dash, she pulled back on the lines, trying to slow Tilly enough to make the corner without overturning. The mare seemed to sense the plan. She slowed and made the turn with the buggy tilting on two wheels. Mary grabbed Hannah and held on to her. Swerving wildly behind the horse, the buggy finally came back onto all four wheels. Before the mare could gather speed again, a man jumped into the road waving his arms. He grabbed Tilly's bridle and pulled her to a stop.

Shouting, he pointed toward an abandoned farmhouse. "There's a cellar on the south side."

Mary jumped out of the buggy and pulled Hannah into her arms. The man was already unhitching Tilly, so Mary ran toward the ramshackle structure. The wind threatened to pull her off her feet. The trees and even the grass were straining toward the approaching tornado. She reached the old cellar door, but couldn't lift it against the force of the wind. She was about to lie on the ground on top of Hannah when the man appeared at her side. Together, they were able to lift the door.

A second later, she was pushed down the steps into darkness.

*Don't miss
AMISH REDEMPTION by Patricia Davids,
available April 2015 wherever
Love Inspired® books and ebooks are sold.*

www.Harlequin.com

*On the wagon train out West, will Ben Hewitt find love
again with Abigail Bingham Black—the woman who
broke his heart six years ago?*

Read on for a sneak preview of Linda Ford's
WAGON TRAIN REUNION,
the exciting beginning of the new series
JOURNEY WEST.

Benjamin Hewitt stared. It wasn't possible.

The man struggling with his oxen couldn't be
Mr. Bingham. He would never subject himself and his
wife to the trials of this journey. Why, Mrs. Bingham
would look mighty strange fluttering a lace hankie and
expecting someone to serve her tea.

The man must have given the wrong command
because the oxen jerked hard to the right. The rear wheel
broke free. A flurry of smaller items fell out the back. A
woman followed, shrieking.

"Mother, are you injured?" A young woman ran
toward her mother. She sounded just like Abigail. At least
as near as he could recall. He'd succeeded in putting that
young woman from his mind many years ago.

She glanced about. "Father, are you safe?"

The sun glowed in her blond hair and he knew without
seeing her face that it was Abigail. What was she doing
here? She'd not find a fine, big house nor fancy dishes

and certainly no servants on this trip.

The bitterness he'd once felt at being rejected because he couldn't provide those things had dissipated, leaving only regret and caution.

She helped her mother to her feet and dusted her skirts off. All the while, the woman—Mrs. Bingham, to be sure—complained, her voice grating with displeasure that made Ben's nerves twitch. He knew all too well that sound. Could recall in sharp detail when the woman had told him he was not a suitable suitor for her daughter. Abigail had agreed, had told him, in a harsh dismissive tone, she would no longer see him.

It all seemed so long ago. Six years to be exact. He'd been a different person back then. Thanks to Abigail, he'd learned not to trust everything a woman said. Nor believe how they acted.

But Binghams or not, a wheel needed to be put on. Ben joined the men hurrying to assist the family.

"Hello." He greeted Mr. Bingham and the man shook his hand. "Ladies." He tipped his hat to them.

"Hello, Ben." Abigail Bingham stood at her mother's side. No, not Bingham. She was Abigail Black now.

Don't miss
WAGON TRAIN REUNION by Linda Ford,
available April 2015 wherever
Love Inspired® *Historical books and ebooks are sold.*

www.Harlequin.com